Danger at Dark

'Foxy, we've got to get away from here!'
William whispered urgently.

Ever since arriving at the mill, William had
often dreamed of running away, returning to
Portsmouth and rescuing Lucy. He would make
a home for them together and become a
carpenter just as his father had been . . .

But this was no time for dreaming. Having
seen Badger's cruel bullying of young Tim,
William knew that he had to escape at once. For
anyone w
Hows Mi

Patricia S
whose sh
actually l
imaginar
both nov
was abou

Danger at Dark Hows

Patricia Sibley

A LION PAPERBACK

Oxford · Batavia · Sydney

For the children of Westmont School

Published by
Lion Publishing plc
Sandy Lane West, Oxford, England
ISBN 0 7459 2697 5
Albatross Books Pty Ltd
PO Box 320, Sutherland, NSW 2232, Australia
ISBN 0 7324 0674 9

First edition 1993

Acknowledgments
Details of the historical note are taken from *Shipwrecks of the
Night* by J.C. Medland, by kind permission of the author.

A catalogue record for this book is available
from the British Library

Printed and bound in Great Britain
by Cox & Wyman Ltd, Reading

Contents

1

Under Cold Green Waves

29 August 1782

At last, the most exciting day of William's whole life, and his sister had to go and lose her temper and delay them starting out. He had tossed and turned half the night in his bunk above Lucy's, in the narrow room Father had fitted up just like on board ship—the Cabin, they called it.

'It's not fair! William's going. Why can't I?' Lucy demanded.

Eight years old with big brown eyes like the dog next door and straight fair hair, Lucy was such a skinny little thing she looked about five. Must be plain dotty to think she could go on board a warship, but there she was, purple with rage, drumming on her father's knees with both small fists, shouting, 'There'll be magic and I'll miss it all!'

'Hey, who's going to get my dinner then, if you join the Navy?' Father asked, his jolly red face beginning to crumple up.

'Oh Father, don't cry,' pleaded Lucy, not sure if

it was a joke or not.

'No dinner, nobody to cook my dinner,' sobbed Father while Lucy tried to smooth away the sad wrinkles on his forehead with her fingers.

'Father, I will stay and get dinner. I will truly. I'll fry the herring and—'

'That's my grown-up girl. Tell you what, we'll ask Mrs Brown to take you down by the castle walls and William and I will wave to you. Then everyone will wonder, who is this grand lady—why, they're even waving to her from the *Royal George*.'

'Grand lady,' Lucy said in tones of awe. She tried a deep curtsey and fell over laughing. Mrs Brown, their landlady, lived downstairs and was known secretly as The Old Dragon, but she had a soft spot for Lucy.

'Come on then, Father. It's gone seven already,' William pleaded.

Father could always find time to manage Lucy, especially since their mother had died two years before, but William was running out of patience, wild to be off. In the end Lucy went downstairs to Mrs Brown and they got away, hurrying along the narrow alleys, and bursting out into the bustle of Portsmouth Hard.

'Can I row, Father?' asked William, as they threaded their way through the crowds.

'I reckon you can keep the look-out today, son.'

As they climbed down the seaweedy steps to the dinghy, William wished for the thousandth time that he was a big brawny chap with springy black hair, like his father, instead of bird-boned and pale like his mother. Never mind, keeping the look-out was a very responsible job, especially with the harbour so full of ships, some riding at anchor and dozens of others setting course between them. Close beneath the big ships the water lay dark green and deep-looking, but the rest shone all blue in the early morning sun.

'There goes the rum boat,' Father shouted, waving at a sloop sailing ahead of them out of the narrow harbour mouth, her white sails shining. Now William did feel sorry for Lucy, for all this glitter and gleam on the water was what she called her 'magic'.

Over to their left, on the port bow, the massive walls of Southsea Castle fell sheer into the sea, guarding the port. That was where Lucy would be with Mrs Brown. She would have a good view. Then they were out of the harbour in a stiff breeze that smelled of fish and seaweed.

William gasped out, 'Oh look, look!' Out in the Solent lay line after line of great ships, the Channel Fleet, all ready to sail to the Mediterranean and free Gibraltar. The thirty-six battleships made a forest of tall masts, while a host of smaller men o' war and merchant ships stood alongside and dozens of smaller boats went to and fro with supplies. Everywhere there were families saying goodbye.

'Look Father, there's the *Victory*—she's enormous!'

William's father, Daniel Brett, grinned, shipped the oars for a moment and gazed around. Then he

9

pointed, 'There she is. That's the *Royal George*.'

Why, she was nearly as big as the *Victory*, three decks high. William had eyes for no other ship now. For a week all his waking hours had been taken up with dreaming of the *Royal George* and finding out everything he could about her. He knew she had captured two Spanish galleons and sunk the Frenchies' *Superbe* at the battle of Quiberon Bay with a single blast of her terrible guns—and any minute now he was going aboard!

Father had an important job to do today. His carpentry was quick and careful. He was often employed on Navy ships, because his work was so good. As soon as William was old enough to hold a knife, his father had brought home scraps of wood and showed him how to carve them into little mice. Baby Lucy loved to hold them. Now he was nearly eleven, and Father had arranged for him to make a repair to a gun carriage on board the warship, while he saw to the watercock.

If Mr Hayles, the head carpenter, approved it, William was going to start working for him and one day be taken on as a proper apprentice. When he became a master carpenter, thought William, he would earn enough for them to have a house right on the quay, instead of their poky lodging up the alley and Lucy would be able to watch her 'magic' shining on the water all day.

Tall and splendid, the ship reared above them, with Admiral Kempenfelt's blue flag flying bravely from the mizzen mast. As they came under the towering bows, William could see the figurehead on the prow high above, not a woman as most ships had, but a pair of galloping horses with riders on their backs. A sailor high in the rigging had seen their little boat approaching and a drum was beaten, an order shouted.

'Look, William, they're beginning to tilt the ship over a bit, so the watercock will come above sea level, for me to get at it,' his father said.

William watched, amazed, as the huge boat started to lean over on one side.

'How do they do it?'

'They move the heavy cannon over to one side and alter the balance,' replied his father. 'The watercock is normally under the water. It lets the water in to clean the ship. But for me to repair it, it's got to be out of the water.'

Other small boats swarmed round, unloading supplies. They carried shot and rum, dozens of casks of water and, to William's surprise, several live sheep. *I could stow away*, William thought. But no, life was too exciting here. It was a good thing his tools were in a canvas bag slung round his neck. That left both hands free to shin up the rope ladder let down for them.

Then at last he was actually standing on the quarterdeck of the *Royal George*, but it was not a bit like he had imagined. He had thought there would be officers snapping out orders and sailors shouting 'Ay, ay, sir,' and dashing off to haul on ropes or climb the rigging. No, it was more like a fairground with wives kissing husbands and children running everywhere, pretending to fire the cannon, laughing and screaming, and pedlars shouting their wares.

William was taken aback when he saw there were other children on board. 'Lucy could have come, then,' he said.

'Ah, she's best where she is, might have got squashed in all this crowd. Come on, better give her a wave like we promised.'

So they shoved their way over to the port side and waved in the general direction of Southsea Castle, though it looked far away and a line of merchant ships lay between them and the castle.

'Buy some ribbons for yer lady, lovely ribbons,' a pedlar shouted at them, pushing his tray of favours under their noses.

Father waved him away. 'Fraid we've got work to do. Over here, William.'

They moved further along the gunwale, through the merry crowd and the fumes of rum, to some scaffolding fixed down the ship's side.

'That's where I'm going down to repair the water-cock, son. You can find me there later on. Now you go down to the first gun deck, make for the starboard side, find Mr Hayles and he'll tell you what wants doing.'

William climbed down to the gun deck. It was much quieter there, and dark after the sea dazzle above. Here sailors were working, for the gun crews were busy hauling the port cannon into the middle of the deck, making the ship lean more and more. Diving out of their way, he soon found Father's friend, Mr Hayles, a tall, solemn man who showed him what to do. He had to cut out a length of rotten wood along the side of a gun carriage and joint in a new length of oak.

As the sailors shouted and heaved the guns, the deck began to slope more steeply. William's hands shook with excitement as he laid out his tools the way his father had showed him. Could he get it right? Would he really become a master carpenter and work on great ships like the *Royal George* every day? The feel of the chisel in his hand calmed him down.

He had just begun to chip away the rotten wood when a loud commotion made him look round. To his surprise, there was his father, pushing through the sailors, shouting something with a look on his face which William had never seen before, a look of fear.

Mr Brett barged his way across to the Lieutenant of the Watch, shouting, 'Right the ship quick or she'll go over! Move the guns back to port.'

'Sir, if you can manage the ship better than I can, you'd better take command,' the officer said sarcastically, looking coldly down his nose.

'But she's rising up, I tell you. Rising from the water on the port side. I was on the scaffolding down there—I could see it happening,' Father cried out desperately. 'Where's the Captain?'

The sailors had seen that Mr Brett was right. Without waiting for an order they began to push the guns back to trim the ship. They had to shove and haul the cannon uphill, for the angle of the deck was growing steeper all the time.

'Send more men,' someone was shouting. In the confusion, William heard his father's voice calling, 'William, get up on deck,' but instead he dropped his tools and ran to help the nearest gun crew, adding his small weight to the whole crowd of men desperately setting their shoulders to the huge weight of iron. As he panted and heaved with the sailors, the gun moved a foot, then another foot. Yes, they were winning. One more frantic heave, but this time it would not budge, however hard they tried.

'Heave ho!'

William shoved with the rest, but the cannon would not budge so much as an inch.

'Look out!' someone yelled.

The gun was falling back on top of them! As William leapt wildly sideways, a man screamed with pain, caught between gun and deck. Further along, other guns were breaking loose, sliding to starboard.

'She's going. She's going over!'

'William, William, where are you?'

'Help, help, she's going!'

'We'll have to jump for it.'

'Father!' William was shouting through the terrible confusion, trying to climb a deck steep as a wall, frantic to find Father, his precious tools forgotten. He could not see him anywhere in the mass of struggling bodies—the sailors had realized it was too late, the ship was going to capsize and they could only try to save themselves. *Get up on deck*, Father had said, but the way was jammed with the struggling crew. He looked wildly round. Water was slopping in fast over the gunports, but it was the only way. He took a deep breath and dived through.

He was sucked down under a cold green wave, down and down. *Ship dragging you down*, said a voice in his head, *get away from it*. His clothes hung heavy and sodden, but he had learnt to swim as soon as he could walk and he struck out and up into a seething mass of struggling sailors, a mess of ropes and wood and barrels, the great ship going down. Father had been up near the bow, so he made towards it or where the bow should have been, trying to raise his head above the swirling water, shouting for Father. Dozens of other voices were crying out and spars and casks bobbed everywhere, threatening to roll over him, bear him down.

'Father!' he managed to gasp, trying to lift his head. In that moment he glimpsed the top of a mast still sticking up above the churning water. *Swim to left, climb up mast, see out over wreck, find Father*, said the tired voice in his head.

He had just enough strength to pull himself up to the topsail halyard block, gasping and choking. He had barely enough breath to shout. Ever such a strong swimmer, Father was, he'd swum right across to the Island once. He was sure to be all right, wasn't he?

At last a small rescue boat came in sight, threading

between a dozen bobbing heads and waving arms, already low in the water with the number of casualties brought aboard.

'Hang on a bit, boy. Got to take the injured first,' shouted the oarsman over his shoulder, busy hauling one more limp body from the sea.

'Find my father!' William shouted back.

One of his legs was trailing in the water and something moved ever so lightly against it. When William looked down he saw a mouse frantically swimming round and round, its eyes bulging with fear. By carefully moving his leg, he brought it up under the small creature. It scrambled up with its last little strength. Reaching down, he picked up the tiny, sodden, furred body and stowed it inside his shirt where the mouse's terrified heartbeat felt like a madly ticking watch against his skin.

Lucy. Lucy loved mice. Had she waved at the ships, had she seen the *Royal George* go over? He could not hang on much longer. *Father, where is he? Arms all aching fire. Going to fall* ... When he looked down, it was to see a sheep swimming placidly past, with a small boy clinging to its back. *Sheep—must be dreaming. So tired ... sleep in the water ... Lucy?* All cold and numb now, hands slipping, his last strength gone, William fell into the cold green waves.

When he came to, William found himself in a vast, grand room, all shining wood, with sunlight pouring through latticed windows onto rows of draggled men, lying on the floor, groaning and crying out. He staggered to his feet, feeling swimmy in the head and cold but driven on. Father must be here somewhere. As the floor tilted slightly he realized he was on board some ship. The man next to him rolled over and was violently sick. Sailors were bending over another man at the far end.

'Father, are you there?' he called softly.

As his head cleared he began to move along the row of victims. One had a deep bloody gash right across his forehead, another lay in a cold sleep from which he might never wake. The last man tried to grab him by the ankle, crying out, 'Help me, help me.' Father was not in that row.

He tried the next: a woman moaning, a little boy unconscious, an old man calling 'Minnie, Minnie', but no Father. *He must be here*, William thought, desperately, *he must*. Not in the next row either. He hurried over to the sailors, officers in grand uniforms.

'Please, sir, where am I, and where's my father?'

A big man with gold braid looked at him.

'Here's one who'll survive, anyway. You're on board the *Victory*, son. Who is your father?'

'Daniel Brett, the carpenter, sir.'

Gold Braid shook his head. 'Could be anywhere, on another ship, taken back to the harbour, even on the Island. Get yourself up on deck and there'll be boats going to Portsmouth.'

On board the *Victory*! At any other time he would have been mad with excitement to be on the great ship. Outside the cabin there were men everywhere, shouting, carrying bodies, shoving him aside.

'Daniel Brett, have you seen Daniel Brett?' but no one had time to listen. On deck he stared up, marvelling at the tall masts towering more than a hundred feet above him. He could tell Lucy he'd been on board the *Victory*. Presently, with half a dozen other survivors, he was rowed along the Solent, into the harbour and set down at the quay. The sun still glittered on the water, making what Lucy called her 'magic', but he hardly noticed.

He'd lost his precious tools; Father would be cross about that. There were people everywhere, lining the harbour, gazing out anxiously across the water, milling round the stone steps as more boatloads came in sight, shouting and calling out names and sobbing. Suddenly the crowd split apart and Lucy shot out of it, big dark eyes in a white face, and threw her arms round him, crying, 'Will, Will, you're all right! Oh, I saw that lovely ship sinking and sinking, and you were on it! I thought I might never see you again, ever.' And a bit later on, after he had hugged her tight, 'Where's Father?'

'Come on Lu, let's go home. I want some dry clothes.'

'But where's Father?' she persisted.

'He'll be along a bit later, I expect.'

When they had hurried back to their lodgings he went to strip off his shirt and felt a small warm bulge against his chest. It was the mouse.

'But when will Father be home?' Lucy was getting fretful. 'Shall I put the herrings on the fire now?'

'Lucy, I've got a present for you.'

She cheered up at once at the mention of a present.

'What? Where? Show me quick,' she cried, dancing up and down.

Mouse had dried out to a fluffy ball of grey fur. He opened sleepy eyes, yawned, stretched his two front paws and whiffled his long silver whiskers, while William told her the story of his rescue.

'Oh brave, darling mouse,' she said gently, cupping her hands round him. 'We must give him a big brave name like . . . like lion or tiger.'

'Tigermouse?'

'Yes, yes, that's it! Now I'll find him some supper and then put him to bed. Come along now, Mr Tigermouse.'

Lucy bustled about, her fair hair shining in the candlelight, lining a box with scraps of rag, putting Tigermouse in the first bed he had ever known. Meanwhile William, suddenly empty with hunger, grilled the herrings on the special brick by the fire, glad of the mouse because it stopped Lucy asking questions for a while. Of course, as the officer had said, Father could have been taken to another ship or even the Isle of Wight. He might be just a bit injured and sent to hospital, but as darkness fell and there was no word, William began to feel dreadfully afraid.

As he undressed he found half a dozen purple

bruises and when he lay down, his body ached all over, yet he couldn't sleep. *Dear God, please send Father home safe.* If—that dreadful if—Father never came back, how would he work and look after Lucy?

Outside, the town was strangely quiet. Before midnight there were usually bands of drunken sailors rollicking past to their ships, singing and shouting, but not tonight. William tossed and turned, trying not to wake Lucy in the bunk below. Turning onto his left side, he tried burrowing into the pillow. Then he heard a small noise, sat bolt upright. Was it Father creeping in so as not to wake them? No, it was only Tigermouse, used to sleeping only in the day, happening to move a shoe as he explored his new home. At four o'clock he heard the watchman crossing the quay, calling, 'Four of the clock and all's well.'

But all was not well. Two days later, Father had still not come home. Wheezing and complaining, Mrs Brown, the Old Dragon, came slowly up the stairs. She had a big white face like a lump of lard, except for her nose which was bright red.

'Here, where's me rent then?' she demanded.

Their money was always kept in a Toby jug on the shelf. William tipped it out on the scrubbed table. Mrs Brown pawed it over and scrabbled the lot into her apron pocket.

'Isn't there any left?' William asked. There always had been before.

'No there is not, and what about next week's?' she said sharply.

'Why, Father'll pay it when he gets back,' Lucy said, surprised.

'You ain't got no father no more.'

'But I'm going to work,' William burst out, before Lucy could realize what she meant. 'Mr Hayles is going to take me on and—'

'Mr Hayles was drowned, and who'd want a little runt like you working for them?' Mrs Brown sneered.

'He's not a r-runt, he's my brother!' Lucy exclaimed, getting red in the face.

'Have you got any aunties or uncles about here?' Mrs Brown went on.

William shook his head.

'Right, I shall want these rooms come Monday then,' she said grimly. 'Course, you could come and stay long o' me, I s'pose—' she said, looking thoughtfully at Lucy—'help with the lodgers a bit.'

'I couldn't stay without William!' Lucy cried.

'That's it, then. Out of here Monday morning, nine o'clock sharp.'

William stared at her, white-faced. With no money, nothing in the world, where could they go?

2
Inside the Iron Gates

Oh no—not leave the Cabin!

William rushed out of Mrs Brown's and down the alley-way to the harbour. Of course he wouldn't be able to get a proper job at once—anything would do just so long as he could pay the rent. He was stopped in his headlong rush by a slow procession crossing the quay, carrying something wrapped in a sheet: more bodies were swept in by every high tide. Somewhere a bell was tolling, solemn and mournful, dong, dong, through the blue summer air.

He went first to a friend of his father's, Mr Burt, another carpenter.

'Plane and chisel for you, Mr Burt? Sweep up the shavings?'

Mr Burt shook his head and turned away. His brother had been on the *Royal George* and was not yet accounted for.

William galloped back to the harbour and found the old fisherman who sometimes told him stories of pirates and great storms at sea.

'Carry your fishboxes up to the market, Uncle Ben? Father . . . Father hasn't come back yet.'

'Neither have hundreds of others,' said the old man sadly, puffing at his pipe. 'I can't do anything for you, lad.'

So he ran to the dockyard gates, but it was chaos there, people rushing in and out, orphaned children like himself but mostly bigger and stronger, all looking for work, or begging from the crowds.

All day William tried. He would do anything to keep a roof over their heads, to save the Cabin, the only security he and Lucy had left—but no one would even listen. All the talk was of the wreck. It was rumoured seven or eight hundred had drowned on the *Royal George*, including Admiral Kempenfelt himself.

There was one other place. Mother used to take them there on the way back from church to give pennies to the mudlarks. The tide was going out now, leaving a glistening expanse of thick brown mud. He went to have a look.

Half a dozen small boys were hanging around, ragged, spotty, listlessly waiting, but today no rich ladies passed by and paused to toss coins and laugh at the entertaining sight of children scrabbling in the mud, desperate for even a farthing. William remembered how Mother would bring what pennies she could spare, and give them straight to the children, telling them to go home and give the money to their mothers. Then she would look at Lucy and William and say, 'Never forget how lucky we are, my loves. You will never have to do anything so dreadful.'

William knew he could not plunge himself into the stinking mud, to be laughed at by nasty sneering people. Mother would have been horrified. There was nothing for it but to go home. His bruises were beginning to ache. Mrs Brown had said they would have to 'go up the hospital' and he knew what that meant: it was nothing to do with sick people, but a place for beggar children. The workhouse*, they called it.

On Monday morning, their few belongings done up in a bundle, Lucy and William said goodbye to the Cabin, the only home they'd ever known. When Mrs Brown hustled her out into the street, Lucy went very quiet and white. Only her special secret kept her from bursting into tears. For of course Tigermouse was going too, travelling in a small bag William had placed around her neck under her smock.

Even now, William desperately hoped that Father might appear, having merely been put out of action for a few days by some knock on the head. He would come rollicking round the next corner, whistling 'Shenandoah', setting everything to rights in a twinkle with his big jolly laugh. But he didn't come.

Mrs Brown led the way. Soon even the streets were strange. What would it be like, the workhouse?

* In Portsmouth the workhouse was called the Hospital—this was a real building.

24

Would the people be kind to Lucy?

They came to a big redbrick building with heavy iron gates. Lucy clutched William's hand very tight and her eyes went big and round. Mrs Brown knocked with a massive iron handle on a tall door that had a very shut look, as if once you were inside you might never get out again. Though the sun still shone, William went all cold. After a noise of bolts and chains being undone, the door opened.

'Two more from the *Royal George*', Mrs Brown said quickly, shoving them inside, then drawing Lucy back to give her a quick kiss.

William bit his lip hard. Of course boys don't cry, but it was a dreadful moment when the door slammed shut on their old life. All around were bare walls and cold-looking stone stairs and passages leading away into the unknown. And Lucy hadn't realized what 'the hospital' meant before. He turned to the small, dark woman who had let them in and said, 'If you please ma'am, this is Lucy Brett and I'm her brother William.'

'Are you now? I'm Mrs Jennet. I suppose I'll have to try and find you beds for tonight at least, though we're dreadfully overcrowded already. You're to go straight before the Board. They're meeting specially this morning because of you *George* lot.' William couldn't see how a board could meet—surely it was a wooden thing you smoothed down with a plane, the way Father had taught him?

'Come along then, down here,' Mrs Jennet was

saying, pushing them ahead of her across a long hallway.

Lucy didn't speak at all, just gazed dumbly round, the hand that was not holding William's creeping up to shield her thin little chest, worrying about Tiger-mouse in his bag.

Outside a large door, a dozen boys and girls stood waiting in line—all ages, from toddlers up to children of eleven or twelve, and all silent. Strange it was, the quiet. There had always been noises outside their lodgings, sailors passing, carts rumbling across the cobbles, fish sellers crying 'mackerel'. They stood behind a white-faced boy with flaming ginger hair. Lucy's hand wandered up to her chest again. She looked worriedly up at William and he knew exactly what she meant. If Tigermouse let out the smallest, smallest squeak, everyone would hear it. He wished he could just worry about a mouse and not about their whole future.

All this time they had been shuffling slowly along nearer to the door: now, almost without realizing, they were at the head of the queue. Then they were pushed inside.

William supposed the board must be the long table which stretched in front of them, made of beautiful shiny wood, perhaps walnut. Later on he learnt that it was the ladies and gentlemen sitting round it who were known as the Board of Governors.

The gentleman in the middle did most of the talking. His white wig contrasted sharply with the

26

stubble of his dark beard. He asked who they were and where they lived and how old they were.

One lady looked carefully at William. 'He doesn't look eleven,' she said, gently. Her blue silk coat was all little pleats and ruffles, her hair done up in such a tall pile on the top of her head, you could have kept Tigermouse in it.

'And what can you do, William?' asked Darkbeard.

'I can read and write, sir. My Mother taught me. And I'm going to be a master carpenter.'

He had thought it all out while they were waiting. If the Board would let him find work and start earning money, he would soon be able to move Lucy out of this cold, unfriendly building. Why, as soon as he had enough money to pay the rent, surely Mrs Brown would let them have the Cabin back again. She did have a soft spot for Lucy, after all.

'Good with your hands, are you, boy?'

'Yes sir, only I lost my carpenter's tools when the *Royal George* went down.'

Darkbeard leant across to a short man, so fat he was almost as round as a ball, and said, 'I think the mill batch, don't you?'

Fatman nodded. 'They'll take him, I should think. Crake likes them small, but he'd easily pass for eight or nine, wouldn't he?'

William was furious. 'I'm ever so strong, sir, even if I do look a bit—short.'

'Good, good,' murmured Fatman, busy writing in a book. 'All the better.' Whatever was a 'millbatch'?

William thought a batch was half a dozen loaves put in the oven to bake together.

'And now the little girl,' Silklady was saying in a sweet, light voice. 'Rather fragile-looking. Better keep her here, don't you think?'

'Crake'll take them at seven,' said Fatman.

'But I've taken such a fancy to her. She looks such a little poppet,' said Silklady, smiling at Lucy.

'I'm William's sister, not a little pop—' Lucy began indignantly, but Darkbeard went straight on speaking. 'As you please, Lady Harriet,' he said, with a sigh.

As they were ushered out, Lucy turned, waved at Silklady and gave her a brilliant smile from her big brown eyes. *She can charm the leg off a chair sometimes*, William thought ruefully, as Lady Harriet waved back. What was going to happen to them now?

There was hardly time to think before they found themselves hit by waves of noise, so loud that Lucy hid her head under his jacket, and he couldn't blame her, for this was the most bewildering place. Before he could sort out what had happened with the Board and whether he was going to be sent away, they found themselves in a huge room with long tables stretching away into the distance and every one lined with children on both sides, all talking, shouting and wolfing down food.

Someone made room for them at the end of one table and soon they were eating soup and hunks of hard bread as fast as the rest. The smell of food made William realize that breakfast at home had been ages ago, in another world, it seemed. Though Lucy gobbled hers down too, he saw her stow some crumbs in a pocket and smiled to himself.

'You for the mill?' shouted his neighbour, the boy with red hair, above the uproar.

'Well, yes, I think so. What does it mean?'

'We'll soon find out, mate. I'm going too. Name's Foxy—you can guess why,' he said with a friendly grin.

'Is it some mill up the river, where we're going to work, then?'

Foxy looked at him as if he were mad. 'Up river! They says it's up country, hundreds of miles away. Making cotton or summat. Still, it might be a lark,' he said cheerfully, mopping up the last traces of soup with a chunk of bread. William couldn't eat any more. He felt choked. *Lucy to stay here all on her own while I'm sent hundreds of miles away? Oh no!* They mustn't lose each other as well as Father and their home.

'Here, Foxy, look after my sister a minute, would you,' he yelled, and rushed away to find someone in charge. He needed to explain how he must stay here to look after Lucy. There was no one about in any of the long echoing passages. But, rounding a corner at speed, he bumped full tilt into Darkbeard.

'Hey, nipper, where d'you think you're off to, eh?' he exclaimed, grabbing William's arm so tight it hurt.

'You'll never get out of here, you know.'

'I—I'm very sorry to have bumped into you, sir.'

'If you do run away, you'll only starve, or have to go and join the beggars and thieves or the mudlarks in the harbour.' The man didn't sound angry, just sad.

'Please, sir, I wasn't trying to run away. I was looking for someone important. Like you,' William added with sudden inspiration.

'Were you now?' The big man was sombrely dressed in a dark coat and breeches. With the extra height of the tall wig, he seemed almost a giant to William. 'What's up then—not enough food?'

William explained about Lucy and how they must stay together.

'Hm. Well, it's done now. It's like this, my boy. We simply haven't got room for you all or even the money to feed you. The *Royal George* going down like that was a shocking thing for the town. So most of the children have to go up to Derbyshire, where they can earn their keep, d'you see?'

'Then can't Lucy come with me, sir? I'll look after her.'

Darkbeard seemed to droop a bit, sighed, and said eventually, 'That pretty little thin gel? Lady Harriet has taken a fancy to your sister and we daren't offend her. She gives us a lot of money.'

'Sir, let me stay in Portsmouth, then. I'll get a job and save up and—'

'Get on back with the other boys. The wagon

30

leaves soon.' Darkbeard's voice had taken on a sudden sharp edge and William saw other men coming into the hall. Hurriedly, the big man pushed something hard and cold into his hand. 'Be off with you now!'

William slunk round a corner, out of sight. In his hand was a silver piece. *Should I run away now?* But he couldn't dash off like that without a word to Lucy. Somehow he found his way back, following the noise that had grown to a real uproar. The children were munching green apples and chucking the cores across the room.

'Tigermouse is all right,' Lucy whispered. 'He's just turned over in his sleep and sort of wriggled a bit and hugged himself like you do when you're all comfy in your bunk.'

'Good. Look, Lucy, I'm going to try and—'

A bell rang out. Instantly everyone stopped talking and throwing apples. Up on a platform at the far end stood Mrs Jennet.

'All the children who came yesterday and today, stand up!' she shouted. They shuffled to their feet. 'Now listen hard. If I call your name, you're going to the mill and you go out of that door there.' She pointed to a door at the end of the hall.

When William heard his name, he knew he had to go. But he had to say goodbye to Lucy, try to explain to her what was happening. He stood up and a tidal wave of boys swept him along. Now they were separated in the jostling crowd.

'Lucy!' he called, but other boys were pushing him forward. 'Mrs Jennet!' *Surely she'll help.* He turned round to get back to her and collided with a tall thin boy.

'Hey, look where you're going, mate!'

'Move along now!' Mrs Jennet was getting cross.

Shoving against the tide of boys, he struggled back at last to Lucy's side. He had hoped that she would not really understand what was happening, but already huge tears were falling down her cheeks, wetting her long hair, and her little face was all pink and swollen with crying.

'William, don't go. Don't go away and leave me,' she sobbed into his shoulder, throwing her arms round his neck so tight that he was nearly throttled.

'Lucy, I've got to go. Just for a little while.'

'No, no, you mustn't!'

'Lu, I'll come back, I promise.'

A heavy hand descended on his shoulder. Mrs Jennet was looking really grim now. He unwound Lucy's arms from his neck, and gave her a last quick hug before he was herded out of the door into a yard and straight onto a shabby old wagon with straw in the bottom. The door was banged shut behind them so there was no chance of a final wave to Lucy and no possible way of escape. William swallowed hard. Now everything that had made up his life, the Cabin and Father and Lucy, were gone ... Almost at once the wagon was clattering out of the yard, heading north into the unknown.

3
Strange Country

The wagon turned away from the sea through streets William had never seen before. It had all happened so quickly, he felt dazed. Like that time he had hit his head on the Cabin's ceiling, sitting up too quickly in his bunk. The Cabin! Would he ever see it again? He stretched up, staring desperately backwards, but the harbour and the small streets around it were already out of sight.

The other children seemed stunned into silence too. Beside him a skinny little boy had actually curled up into a tight ball with his eyes shut. The fair hair and bird-thin bones reminded him painfully of Lucy. How could he leave her like this? He turned to the boy on his other side, about his own age, the one with a sharp freckled face and a shock of red hair.

'D'you know where we're going, Foxy?'

'The driver says we're going to Dark Hows. It's a mill,' said Foxy, running a hand through his hair so that it stood up straight like a brush. They were climbing up a steep chalk road now, over the downs, pulled by a single big brown horse. You could look back and see the harbour and the Solent, even the long hills of the Island. The sight made him feel choked. It all looked so far away already.

'Was your father on the *Royal George*?' William asked.

Foxy shook his head. 'Haven't got a father—he sloped off years ago, before I remember. It was my mother. She was on board selling doughnuts. They say there were eight hundred drowned altogether.'

'I was on board.'

'You never were!' Foxy eyed him with some respect. By the time William had told all his adventures they had reached the summit and the wagon came to a halt. The driver, a gruff old man, face half-hidden in grey whiskers, turned round and stared at them from under a large brown hat.

'Don't any of you nippers think you can go skiving off. I can count fifteen with the best. Next time there's a bit of a climb, you can get out and walk. By then you'll be too far away to go running off back home.' He turned back to take up the reins again, then shouted, 'Hey, you!' flourishing his whip, as a boy jumped down from the wagon. It was the little skinny creature who had seemed asleep.

'S'all right, mister, just want to see your hoss,' he called up cheerfully, running round to the tall mare and reaching up his hand with an apple core flat on the palm. Soft lips came down, took it gently. 'She's lovely,' the boy said, tiny beside the great shaggy fetlocks. 'What's her name?'

'Georgina. After the king, sort of,' said the wagoner, softening a shade. 'Come on. Get back in now.'

'I'm Charlie,' said the boy, settling down beside William. 'My Granpy had hosses. D'you think there's hosses in Heaven for him? 'Cos he won't like it otherwise.'

William hadn't given Heaven a thought, though Mother had said she was going there when she got so thin and pale and coughed all night. So if Father had really drowned, he would be there too and they would be ever so excited to find each other again. He remembered how, even if Father had been away for only a day, he would rush into the kitchen and give Mother a big hug and waltz her round and round the kitchen table singing one of his sea-shanties.

Hot sun beat down on the wagon: some children lay asleep in the straw whilst one snivelled into a dirty rag.

'So you're not from the *Royal George* lot,' Foxy said to Charlie.

'No. Me Granpy kept the White Lion with all the stables. He's always looked after me, 'cos I never had no mother and father. He went out to give our Caesar his oats on Sunday and he fell down dead in the yard.'

Charlie sighed, then he brightened up again. 'Hope there's hosses where we're going. I'm good with hosses.' Then he curled up again and went to sleep.

But William couldn't sleep in spite of the heat and the rhythmic clop-clop of the horses' hooves. Where were they going to and why? As the dusty green hedges slipped past, mile after mile, he felt like crying out, 'Stop, stop. I'll never get back to Lucy if you go any further!' But apart from occasional rests for the horse they didn't pause, not even when the sun had gone down and the first stars had come out, chilling the air.

Georgina was evidently tiring. She ambled slowly through a village where lights glowed from the cottage windows. William looked right into one where the shutters had not been closed and saw a family just sitting down to supper, mother, father and three boys round a candlelit table, all cosy and homely... At last they turned off the road and stopped.

'Come on out, then,' shouted the wagoner and they climbed down, cramped and stiff, into the yard of the Green Dragon. 'You can kip in with the horse and I'll get you a bite to eat. There's a trough over there.'

Georgina already had her long nose in the stone trough. When she'd had a long drink, the boys thrust in their hands, splashing water over their heads. Then, gasping from the cold, they drank from cupped hands, until the wagoner said, 'That's enough, then. Come on over here.' He had lit a lantern and they followed him across the yard to the stables.

'You can settle down there,' he said, pointing at a big pile of hay at the far end. The other end was divided into stalls for horses. 'Now then!' He hung the lantern from a beam and slowly looked them over, finally pointing at the tallest boy, a thin, beaky chap called Tim, and Foxy.

'You two. See everybody gets a fair share for supper, and you might get an extra bit of summat. And see nobody tries to slope off, or you'll get a taste of this.' He waved the long whip still in his hand. Then, with a last grim stare from under the wide-brimmed hat, he stumped off to unharness Georgina.

'Here you are, boys,' sang out a warm, friendly voice and in came a fair young woman, all pink and gold, carrying a big tray which she set down on top of some barrels. 'Now come and help yourselves and if you want more, just ask me for it. I'm Mrs Lane. I'll bet you're half starved, you poor little things.'

They fell on the food, big hunks of crusty new bread yellow with butter, slices of delicious crumbly cheese, apples and a big jug of creamy milk. Tim, the tall, thin boy the wagoner had put in charge, made sure that they all had fair shares.

'Please, ma'am, could you tell us where we are?' William asked.

'Why, you're in Chilton. But 'tis only a little tiddy place,' Mrs Lane said. 'Tomorrow you'll be coming to Oxford. Now, that's a great big place all full of splendid buildings.'

William wanted to keep her there. It was comforting just to be near someone cheerful and kind, but he couldn't think of anything else to ask, he was so tired. Somewhere behind them, Georgina clopped slowly in and was settled in a stall.

'Save us your apple cores,' Charlie said.

Foxy seemed to have disappeared, but by the time they had all stretched out on the hay, he was back again. He counted the bodies, grunted and flopped down beside William. The hay was a bit tickly, but it smelled nice and was nearly as soft as his feather bed at home in the Cabin. No, best not think about that. It hurt too much.

'Where've you been?' he whispered to Foxy.

'Talking to the old man. Took him an extra bit of bread and cheese. Says he takes a wagonload of kids up north every week to work in these great big places called mills, where there's machines that make cotton.'

'What do we do there, then?' William asked.

'Get shut in all day and have to keep the machines going, he said, though he's a bit vague about it.'

William looked round the shadowy stable, its half door open to the stars. A hoof thudded in a stall. Other boys were whispering together. The air smelled of hay and horse.

'I don't fancy being shut in.'

'No, me neither. He says you work awful long hours, too.'

'Then we'll earn more money,' William said hopefully. Perhaps he'd soon be able to save enough to get back to Portsmouth.

'He says there's some mills where they treat you decent. And some bad mills.'

'And which is ours?'

'It's called Dark Hows. He wouldn't say much about it,' Foxy whispered.

A toe prodded William in his ear. 'You two are to shut up,' hissed Tim, so at last they curled up and slept.

By the time bossy Tim was shaking them awake, the day was already sunny and promised to be warm. They ran out and plunged their heads in the horse trough, coming back to find Mrs Lane setting down a tray for breakfast. This time the bread was spread with butter and thick fruity jam as well.

'Gallons and gallons of gooseberry jam I made,' Mrs Lane said, beaming at them, her smiling eyes as blue as her apron. 'Tuck in now. You'll have a long day ahead of you.'

'Will we get to the mill today?' Foxy asked her.

Her pretty mouth pursed up at mention of the mill. 'It's still a long way to Derbyshire. You'll have more nights on the road, I reckon,' she said eventually. 'Here, have some more milk.'

Soon a different horse, coal-black Milly, was being backed between the wagon shafts. William didn't want to leave the Green Dragon. Mrs Lane was a reminder that there were kind and cheerful people in the world still, but Tim was already lining them up brusquely in the sunny yard. You could tell a bit of responsibility had really gone to his head.

'Get in line there! Stand still! How can I count you if you keep wandering off? Hey, Foxy, you're supposed to be helping me,' he was shouting, a red spot appearing on each cheek. 'Now then, one, two . . .' Milly let out a loud whinny and pawed the ground. '. . . thirteen, fourteen. There's one missing!'

'Forgot to count yerself,' said Foxy.

'I did not. I did not!' The red spots were fading into panic white. 'Who's missing? We've got to find him.'

William and Foxy knew perfectly well who was missing and where he would be, so they dashed back across the yard to the stables.

'Charlie! Come on out. It's time to go,' William shouted.

No reply. Nothing moved in the gloom except Georgina, who, resting in her stall, turned her head with an inquiring look.

'Look in the stalls and I'll prod through the hay,' Foxy said.

William went along the row of stalls, peering into each. In the last one a youth was grooming the tail of a grey mare and whistling 'Greensleeves'.

'Have you seen a little fair boy?' William asked him. The youth shook his head without dropping a note. 'He's not here,' William called to Foxy who was panting with the effort of turning over all the hay.

'Must be somewhere outside, then.'

William ran across to the inn door and knocked hard. Mrs Lane appeared at once. 'I know. You want some more of my gooseberry jam,' she said with her warm smile.

'No, no. It's Charlie. Have you seen him any-where?' William asked urgently. 'He's skinny and small.'

'Oh no, my dear, I haven't. Hasn't run off, has he? They do try it on sometimes and you can't blame them, can you?'

William and Foxy looked at one another, taut with anxiety. Whatever would happen to the little chap all alone in strange country like this? Suddenly Tim burst between them, eyes popping, frantic.

'Where is he? Where is he? The man's doing up the last buckle on the harness and then we'll have to be off,' he shouted.

'He's vanished into thin air,' Foxy said flatly.

'Find him! We've got to find him or we'll be whipped!'

William had a hunch. He dashed back into the shadowy stable, unable to see anything for a moment after the dazzle outside. He went straight to Georgi-na's stall, its entrance almost blocked by her massive hindquarters.

'Charlie!' Nothing stirred. William wasn't fright-ened of horses but had never had much to do with them. Still, he had got to make sure. He squeezed between the wooden partition and her brown flank, murmuring, 'All right, Georgina, all right, girl,' till he could peer underneath. Between the four great hooves was a straw-covered bundle.

'Charlie! I know that's you. Look, you've got to come out quick. We're all ready to go off.'

The bundle twitched, muttered, 'I's not coming.'

'Charlie, you can't stay here, all on your own.'

'I heard you saying about being shut up in a horrible old factory, and I's not coming.'

William was in despair. If he tried to drag Charlie out, they were bound to upset Georgina. A hoof that size could easily kick you to death. Fetching Foxy wouldn't be any good, either. There was no room for two of them. Already the mare was beginning to twitch uneasily, looking round at him with a rolling eye.

'Charlie, come on. If you don't come out of there this minute, Tim and Foxy'll be whipped to death . . .' No harm in laying it on a bit. Golden dust motes danced in a shaft of sunlight streaming through the doorway: a pigeon croo-crooed from the roof. Charlie did not stir. If anything, the bundle huddled itself smaller. 'Oh well, I'll just have to go and get the wagoner to come and drag you out, I suppose.'

'No! No! You wouldn't do that, Willum.' A white face peeked out of the straw.

'I would. But,' William added craftily, 'if you come out quick, I'll give you three apple cores for Milly. You'll love her. She's in the shafts already.'

At last Charlie began to uncurl. 'Be careful!' William exclaimed. He knew enough about horses to realize that each of Georgina's shaggy hooves was shod with a heavy iron shoe. But once he had squeezed carefully out of the stall, Charlie appeared beside him, unharmed.

42

'Give us the apples, then.'

From the yard, Foxy's red head was visible in the distance, as he scouted the orchard of the inn.

'Foxy, come on!' William yelled.

The wagon was waiting, full of boys, the wagoner holding his reins at the ready, his face black as thunder. Seeing Charlie, he roared out, 'Where you been, you little rat?' so loudly that five pigeons were startled off the roof.

Charlie skipped straight over to the horse.

'Wus only getting apples for Milly,' he said cheerfully. 'Lovely hoss, ain't she? You must be ever so proud of her,' he said, grinning up into the furious face. Shining black Milly stooped her noble head for the apple cores, then blew softly in his ear.

'Get in there!' roared the old man, but not quite so loudly or so angrily.

Charlie tumbled into the wagon, settled down by William and the cart creaked into motion between the dusty hedges.

'Here, you,' said bossy Tim, sitting up importantly. 'Don't you go running off again. I could have got into terrible trouble, I'll have you know and all because of a little whipper-snapper like you.'

'Shut up,' William said. 'We got him back for you, didn't we? Fat lot of help you were, sitting on your tail in the wagon.'

'Who are you telling to shut up?' and Tim lurched across the straw, red-faced, fists up.

'Oh look! Look!' Foxy cried, pointing over the left

side and at once they all scrambled across, eager for anything new.

'What is it? What d'you see?' asked Charlie.

'It was a blooming great rat and . . . and two little ones,' Foxy said, peering back. 'Jumped in the hedge just as we went by.'

They all slumped back into the straw.

'I never saw a rat,' Tim murmured suspiciously.

William knew very well that there never had been a rat, that Foxy had simply averted a fight. He looked at the freckled face beside him with respect. Here was a chap who knew his way about the world. Tim had subsided back into his place in the opposite corner.

'Thanks, mate,' William whispered.

Foxy grinned. 'See a rat for you any time,' he whispered back.

William felt better, as if a weight had fallen from his shoulders. He had a friend. Whatever happened at Dark Hows, Foxy would be there to share it. There seemed no way he could get back to Lucy at the moment, so he must accept what came and make the best of it. Mother often used to say that a lot. *Learn to make the best of it, son.*

He sat up, looked around. After all, he'd never had a chance to travel before. It was strange. Green fields stretching away as far as you could see. He'd never been land-locked before. Always the sea had been there, shining with the glitter Lucy called her 'magic', or angry, roaring and green. The sun lay on the land, golden and hazy, and all the leaves looked tired, ready to drop soon. Now dusty hedges were giving way to buildings. They had to stop for a handsome carriage drawn by four matching greys, the coachman high on his seat giving them one disdainful glance.

'Must be Oxford,' William said, nudging Foxy. He had never seen a town like this. Portsmouth was all higgledy-piggledy, but in this street all the buildings were of yellowy stone, carved and pinnacled with soaring windows and tall towers. 'Like castles. Or palaces,' he said, overawed, craning his neck to see more.

'Colleges,' Foxy said. 'They're where clever chaps go to study books.'

'D'you have to be rich as well?'

'Spec so.'

They gazed around, drinking it all in. Here and there you could glimpse wide green gardens and huge old trees through archways in the high stone walls.

Suddenly Tim sat up and said, 'I'm coming here when I'm older.'

'What, to a college?' Foxy asked, disbelieving.

'If I work really hard. You have to know Latin, of course.'

Nearly all the boys were staring at Tim now.

'D'you really know Latin?' William asked. 'Go on, say some.'

Tim's normally pale face had gone strawberry pink. He mumbled something.

'Go on, say it again. We couldn't hear,' Foxy demanded.

'*Hic, haec, hoc,*' Tim pronounced.

The boys took it up, chanting proudly, 'Hick, hike, hock!'

'What's it mean, then?' William asked, feeling a new respect for bossy Tim, in spite of himself. But Charlie had woken up in time to admire a handsome chestnut pony pulling a trap and a piebald tethered to a railing.

'Look, hosses, hosses!'

Steeples, churches, clocks chiming. William wished Lucy could see it all. The farthest he'd ever been from home before was when Father had rowed them across to the Isle of Wight, the Island as everyone called it. They'd landed at Ryde, but it wasn't much of a place, just a few fishermen's shacks and a lot of mud, nothing grand and exciting like this. As they began to leave the town behind, he craned round to see the very last stones of golden Oxford.

'Foxy, how come you know so much about colleges and everything?' he asked, as they settled down again, jogging along the bumpy road through the stubble fields.

'Don't reckon I'm ever going to Oxford,' Foxy said wryly, chewing a piece of straw. 'Don't know any Latin. Just I've met lots of people, picked up bits of this and that.'

'Where did you live?'

'In Fish Street. Mother had a baker's shop, ever so small, but busy, and we lived over the top. My mother used to get up at four every morning to light the oven, and I used to go along the shore to see what wood had come in on the night tide, before anybody else got there. There always had to be enough to light the oven for next day.'

'Did you make bread too?'

'No. I used to go out delivering after that. Some quite grand houses like that Lady Harriet's wanted Mother's bread and doughnuts. Used to talk to everybody, always rushing off somewhere and sort of looking after Mother. It was . . . it was all right . . .' Foxy seemed to run out of words and William knew he was remembering a good time now vanished forever.

That night they slept at the Hare and Hounds. It sort of hypnotized you, jogging along, jogging along, so you stopped thinking, William decided. The next night it was the Dog and Duck, then the Royal Oak. Charlie fell in love with all the horses in turn, Marigold, Martha and Daisy.

The land was changing now, heaving up into green hills patterned with white stone walls that seemed to shine through the grey air, for the weather had turned misty.

'All out,' shouted the driver, when a really steep hill reared before them, and they tumbled out, whooping and yelling, glad to stretch their legs.

'Get round in front so I can see what yer up to,' he shouted.

'Yes, come along now,' said Tim, bossily. But no one took any notice of him.

Daisy, an elderly chestnut with cream mane, tail and feathers over her feet, clopped slowly on. Tall blue flowers grew along the roadside, and high above, the green hills broke off here and there into steep white cliffs. Foxy looked at William, a gleam in his eye, and without a word, they began to run, racing for the summit of the hill.

'Hey, you boys, come back! You know you're not supposed...' Tim's voice faded away behind them.

The hill was long and steep. They reached the top at last in a dead heat, puffing and panting, and fell sprawling on the grassy verge.

'Look, there's miles more,' William exclaimed, waving ahead over a sea of green hilltops, all wild and exhilarating. Little birds were spiralling up through the evening air, singing.

'Larks,' Foxy said, his freckles glowing from the run. Suddenly he sat up, clutching his pockets, face sharp with anxiety.

'What's up?' William asked.

Foxy fumbled around his jacket and at last heaved a sigh of relief.

'It's all right. Cor, thought for a minute I'd dropped it. Don't look much, do it?'

On his hand lay what William thought at first was a stone, round and brown, but when he touched it, his fingers met something rough and light.

'What is it?'

Foxy shoved it back in his pocket. 'It's an Isle of Wight doughnut. Mother came from over there, see.

She had this special recipe, small they were, with currants in, lovely hot. Nobody else in Portsmouth made them like that.'

'And that's the last one?'

As Foxy nodded, the wagon climbed slowly into view. The old man gave them a bit of a stare, but he liked Foxy, who gave him titbits for his horses.

'Couple of hours,' he said tersely, as they climbed back in.

'What's he mean?' asked Charlie.

'He means in two hours we shall arrive at Dark Hows, our destin-destination,' said Tim importantly, unfortunately stumbling over the long word and turning a delicate shade of pink.

Dark Hows... William didn't want to arrive. He would have just liked to chunter on day after day in the wagon with Foxy and Charlie and a new world going gently by, full of surprises.

Night had fallen when the wagon came to a final halt and the wagoner shouted, 'Dark Hows, Dark Hows! All out!'

There was a cold sound of rushing water and a huge, more solid darkness, blotting out the stars and looming over them, which must be the mill itself. William looked at Foxy and shivered. What was going to happen to them at Dark Hows?

4

Inside Dark Hows

The great dark building loomed above them. A door opened in the nearest wall, and the wagoner herded them into a long, low room lit by a single guttering candle. In its dim light William could just make out rows of sleeping bodies wrapped in grey blankets, lying on a thin layer of straw.

'You're late, keeping me up all hours. You'll all be fined,' a voice snapped out of the darkness. They turned to see a big plump youth lounging in the doorway behind them, dark-haired but for a startling streak of white.

'Well, Daisy got tired with having to climb all them—' Charlie started to explain, but a big hand came down and cuffed his ear.

'Shut up, you. Don't you go answering back your old friend Badger—he don't like it, see?' Mean black eyes gleamed in the smoky light. 'Get a blanket and settle down. You're waking the others.'

With all the fresh air and hill climbing, William's stomach had been gurgling with emptiness for hours.

He looked at Tim, waiting for this scholar to take the lead, but the tall boy was gazing around, silent and appalled, so he asked, 'Where's our supper, then?'

'Oh, where's our supper,' said Badger, trying to put on a la-di-da voice mocking William's southern drawl. 'Where's our chicken and strawberries, our port wine? Well, here it is!'

Reaching up to a high shelf he produced a plate of bread, tossing the chunks onto the floor so that the boys had to scrabble for them like dogs. William's piece tasted sour and stale, but he wolfed it just the same. He looked down to see little Charlie beside him, swaying with tiredness on his feet, staring at his hunk as if it might bite him.

'Come on, Charlie, it's better than nothing,' he whispered, breaking off a bit for him.

'Nighty-night then,' said the Badger creature in his nasty, sneering way. 'And don't be late in the morning. Mr Crake don't like that at all.' Then he slammed the door behind him.

Before William had properly settled on the thin straw in a foul-smelling blanket, the candle guttered and went out so they were in a bleak darkness, full of snuffles and whimpers.

The floor's so hard, I'll never sleep, William thought, turning and tossing. Was this how life was to be for always, a cold hard floor to sleep on, stale bread and a bully-boy over them? As usual at night he thought about Lucy, how he could get back to her and if she was being looked after all right, and said a quick prayer, *Please, God, take care of Lucy*. Tonight he desperately needed some care himself, and he remembered kind Mrs Lane with her gooseberry jam. And Mother. She always said God would look after you, wherever you were. At least Lucy would have a bed, so perhaps he needn't trouble God about her tonight. In the end he was just deciding to ask God to look after them all, when something brushed his face and he shot bolt upright, sure it was a rat.

'S'only me,' Charlie whispered. 'Sorry.'

He patted the little bundle. Foxy slept on his other side, so at least he was in the middle of his gang. Perhaps that was God's answer, reminding him that he had friends. As he was just drifting off, a fearful deep baying broke out somewhere in the distance, as if a huge dog were on the loose. Then at last he slept.

Almost at once, it seemed, a voice was shouting through his dreams, 'Wake up! Get up! Come on, you lazy swine!' Then something kicked him in the ribs and William awoke.

It was still pitch dark. By the light of a lantern he could see a man's face staring down at him, a sharp white face, eyes staring from black hollows.

'Get into the mill, the lot of you.'

In his hand the man held a long stick. All around in the darkness William could sense other children struggling out of their blankets and a low, fearful whisper crept along the air, 'It's Crake—it's Crake! He's got the billy-roller!'

This was the fearsome stick he carried, made of cold, gleaming iron, with a sharp point at one end. William was too cold and stiff to move quickly, but the chill air of the yard outside really woke him up. Close by came the sound of a river running fast and a wind moaning in trees.

'Foxy,' he whispered. 'Why have we got to get up in the middle of the night?'

'Must be nearly five o'clock,' Foxy whispered back. 'That's when the day shift starts up, Rob says. He's been here six months. He reckons you got to look out for that Crake too. He's the Master.'

The sky was just beginning to lighten now, so that William could make out the roof of a huge building towering over them before they were herded across the yard and into the mill.

He had been afraid when the *Royal George* sank and barrels threatened to run him down and drown him under the cold green waves. But now he was so scared his knees went all weak. The place was full of great machines, whizzing and clattering and roaring and worst of all, moving about. One seemed to rush right at him so that he had to jump aside.

'Here, you. Don't stand about gawping. You're to keep this part clean. Along there, down here. Spotless, mind, and don't let me catch you standing about idle again,' shouted the youth called Badger. William grasped the broom that was shoved at him.

All right then, he would work, harder than anybody else. They would see how good he was, give him a better job, so he would earn more money. Then he would save it all up until there was enough to make a home for Lucy. The silver piece the man at the workhouse had given him would surely get him back to Portsmouth? A picture flashed into his mind just for a second—tall ships moored in the shining harbour—then he set to work with the broom.

The building was huge, bigger even than the church that Mother had taken them to every Sunday. All around, children smaller than himself scurried to and fro, some of them no bigger than Lucy, nipping between the snapping monsters of spinning machines, sweeping up, tying broken threads, heaving baskets of bobbins about. In the distance, Charlie struggled to sweep with a broom handle that came above his head. Foxy was behind him somewhere.

At first it seemed easy, just to keep the floor clean, but as the machines clacked to and fro, the air was filled with tiny threads that got in his eyes and up his nose, making him sneeze and settling everywhere in clouds of fluff. As the first shock of noise and strangeness wore off he was able to look around while he swept and see what was happening.

The machines were big wooden frames that moved to and fro on heavy iron wheels, stretching the threads of cotton. They couldn't really attack you. Overhead, long belts whizzed around more wheels, bringing power to the machines, driven by the water from the river, he supposed. Some children raced about the floor tying ends of cotton as soon as they snapped off the whirring bobbins. Soon he was sweating hot, but did not dare take his jacket off because of the precious silver piece in his pocket. Suddenly a violent shove spun him sideways and he looked fearfully into Crake's snapping black eyes. William's heart was filled with fear as the angry man stood over him.

'Get that cleaned out proper before it clogs the machine, or you'll get a lovely taste of the billy-roller,' the man hissed down at him, pointing with his dreaded iron stick under the nearest machine, before he strode away.

William grabbed up his broom, anxious to do better, but the handle was not long enough to reach right under. He looked wildly round to see how the others managed. Next to him a dark-haired girl was diving right under the frame, whipping out the dust before the machine came shooting back. He would have to do that then, crawl right under.

In the black tunnel there was just room to move with the broom. He hated dark, shut-in places, and could feel himself turning all cold and dizzy. He must get out before the machine came back or he'd be squashed, but the sides were shutting him in, trapping him, just like a mouse in a tunnel... Then he thought of something. Down there in the dark and the fluff and the danger, where no one could see him, William grinned to himself and his head cleared.

Just pretend you're Tigermouse, he said to himself. So he whiffled his imaginary whiskers, switched his tail and scampered out of the way of the machine as

Tim trudged past, heaving along a huge wheeled basket piled high with white fluffy stuff—the raw cotton, he supposed, before it was spun. Tim rolled his eyes and William gave a quick nod, all they dared do: it seemed a long way from Oxford. Just then a bell rang and everyone stampeded for the door shouting, 'Breakfast, breakfast!'

Out in the yard they had to queue up and file past the door of the building where they slept to collect a bowl of porridge. Thin, watery stuff it proved to be, but he was so hungry, he gulped it down, standing there with Foxy, looking round the yard. Charlie slumped down against the wall, whimpering, 'I's tired, I's so tired,' and Tim queued silently with the rest.

The huge stone mill and its outbuildings walled in two sides, broken-down old cottages took up a third, and behind them ran the river, fast and clear in its rocky gorge, channelled into a leat so that its power could turn the massive wheels which worked all the machinery inside. William stared longest at the river. He thought of all that water racing to the sea.

'Where is the sea, d'you reckon?' he asked Foxy.

'Dunno, mate,' said Foxy. But the big boy with the white-streaked hair had overheard. Badger came lounging over to them, grinning all over his fat face. 'You want to look out for that Badger. He's Crake's creep, Rob says,' Foxy muttered.

'Where's the sea? Where's the sea?' Badger said loudly. 'This yer nipper wants to know where the sea is!' He slapped his fat thighs and roared with laughter. Some of the others joined in. They might not see the joke, but they were all afraid of Badger, who had plenty to eat and wore better clothes than everyone else. They were said to be presents from Crake, given to Badger for his spying.

William would not be cowed, though. 'Come on then, where is the sea?' he asked stoutly.

'Oh, just down the road,' Badger said, hands in pockets. Just for one second, William saw greeny-blue waves crashing onto shingle in a flurry of foam. Could it really be so close? 'Just down there,' Badger jeered, pointing along the valley. 'Only about a hundred miles. Two hundred miles, that's all!'

'Is there a harbour, when you get there, then?' William went on doggedly. There would be boats in a harbour, perhaps even one sailing for Portsmouth.

For a moment, Badger was taken aback and Tim said, into the silence, 'You don't really know, do you?'

Badger's coarse laugh echoed back from the enclosing walls. 'Course I know. Got to be a harbour, if there's the sea,' he sneered.

But any Portsmouth boy who was listening guessed at once that Badger didn't really know what a harbour was, had maybe never even seen the sea. Badger had lost face, and he knew it. He wouldn't forget who had brought that about, either. Foxy moved protectively up beside William as Badger glared at him, but at that moment a bell clanged and they had to hurry back inside the mill.

'You want to look out for that Badger,' Foxy whispered. 'I reckon he's got it in for you and Tim.'

A machine rumbled towards William as he ran to his corner, grabbed up his broom, determined once more to be good at his job. This time the noise and heat and sweeping seemed to go on for ever, though when at last they stopped, it was only twelve by the mill clock. William's arms felt as if they might fall off. Lining up for food, he found himself behind one of the experienced girls, Jill, who changed bobbins. Skinny she was and cowed-looking, but at least she might answer some of the questions that had been seething in his head all the time he'd been sweeping.

'Jill, how much longer do we go on working?'

She looked furtively round to see if anyone was listening, then said, 'Till eight o'clock usually, unless there's a rush on. Then it could be past nine.'

'You mean, another eight hours!' he exclaimed. 'But we've been on since dawn!'

'Sh! Keep your voice down.'

'Charlie won't be able to keep on working like that. He's nearly asleep now,' William said indignantly, looking at the white-faced little boy slumped against the wall, too tired already to line up for his dinner.

'Then Badger will get his whip out or Crake'll be at him with his billy-roller,' Jill said.

'Oh no!' He had a sudden thought. 'Look, could you look after him a bit?'

Her dull eyes lit up for a moment. 'I got a little brother at home.'

'Now you've got one here as well, then,' William said. He went over to Charlie with a piece of bread and dripping.

'Come on, mate. Pretend you're Daisy and this is your nosebag.'

'Wish I was Daisy, trottin' along through the fields,' Charlie said, taking a mouthful. 'When we goin' back, Willum?'

But at that moment Rob dug William in the ribs. William recognized the older boy who had warned Foxy about Badger. 'Time for work,' said Rob curtly.

As they crossed the yard William asked Rob, 'What do we earn?' Rob stared at him as if he were mad. 'I mean,' stuttered William, 'what wages do we get at the end of the week?'

Rob's skin was flaky and greyish like a mushroom. He coughed all the time and his eyes were as grey and lifeless as the pebbles on Southsea beach.

'Just a few pennies, depends how many fines you got,' he said dully, 'and you won't get it till end of the month.'

A few pennies! What a dreadful place this was, William thought, picking up the broom once more. All the children who had been here any length of time looked thin and dull and fearful, like Rob and Jill. The only good thing was that Lucy had not come here with him.

As the hot dreary hours dragged on, the constant rattle and bang gave him a headache. His shoulders ached from the monotonous sweep-sweep-sweeping.

His back ached with stooping. Soon he was one long ache all over. The drifting threads of cotton made him cough like everybody else, till his throat was rough and sore. He longed for a breath of cool air or, like Daisy, to dip his head in a horse trough.

Supper was thin soup and hard bread. When at last the endless-seeming shift was over, William fell onto the hard straw straight into a black pit of sleep.

5

A Bad Dream

As days passed like bad dreams, William was at first too dazed and exhausted and hungry to think, as if he had become a mere sweeping machine. On Sundays they had to clean the real machines in the mill, but then they were free. Some of the local children, like Jill, went home.

The first Sunday after they arrived, the Portsmouth children were lying in the midday sun in the yard, too tired for anything but sleep. William curled up on a sack next to Foxy and fell asleep, but was woken from a jumbled dream about sawing wood that kept jumping about, by Tim having a violent coughing fit.

At first some of the boys had teased Tim, remembering how he had appeared bossy and superior on the journey from Portsmouth. They called 'Hick, hike, hock,' after him, but he hardly seemed to know they were there now, let alone mind what they said, so they had given up. William guessed the tall thin boy had come from some better-off home than the rest of them, so that Dark Hows had been even more of a shock to him.

William lay there wondering drowsily about the Cabin, and who was in it now, and what Lucy was doing. He didn't really know enough about the workhouse to picture her life at all. It must be better than this, though. Perhaps she helped in the kitchen, peeling potatoes or something.

Turning over, William began to tell himself a story about Lucy, as a way of being with her. That pretty Lady Harriet with all her silks and ribbons had taken a fancy to Lu. Well then . . . *One day when his sister was peeling apples in the kitchen, a girl ran in to say that Mrs Jennet wanted her. So Lucy dawdled off, afraid she must have done something bad, but Mrs Jennet was all beaming smiles and said she had a lovely surprise for her. Lucy at once exclaimed 'William!' so Mrs Jennet had to explain that it was not her brother and started to brush her long fair hair. Lucy stamped her foot and said if the surprise was not William, she didn't care what it was, but before she could burst into a howl of rage, Mrs Jennet whisked her off to the front door where a splendid coach was waiting, drawn by two tall white horses, with a footman holding the door open—for her! So Lucy drew herself up as tall as tall and . . . and . . .* William drifted back into sleep.

When he awoke, Tim was sitting up, staring at the river.

'Used to go to church on Sundays,' he murmured.

'Me too. When Mother was alive.'

'My brother Marcus was going to be a priest. He was the clever one.' Tim turned to him, eager to talk to someone who wouldn't laugh. 'He—he taught me a few little bits of Latin.'

'Mother and I used to take my sister and sit her between us so she would behave herself,' William said. 'She thought God lived in a little house behind the altar.'

'Marcus said God was inside people.'

When they were going to bed that night, Charlie dug him in the ribs, eyes shining and whispered, 'That girl Jill went home for the weekend and brought me back a li'l treacle tart!'

William tried to tell himself some more of the Lucy story, but Tim was coughing away like an old dog barking, so he couldn't concentrate, and in the end he fell asleep.

Slowly he grew used to the long hours, the heat, noise, and wretched food, and came out of his daze. By the end of the second week he knew the routine and realized what it had done to the children who had been there longer. They were cowed and dirty, thin and spotty, could no longer think for themselves. He wouldn't *ever* get like that! He would run away from Dark Hows!

Once he had made the great decision, work was not so boring, even on Monday with a whole week of slaving ahead. Sweep, sweep, sweep. As long as he kept that up with his hands, he could be planning in his head. Would Foxy come with him? He must.

Running away with Foxy and all his knowledge of the world would be a real adventure. According to his stomach it must be nearly dinner-time. He would try to get a minute alone with Foxy so they could talk. Should they take Charlie with them? He looked across to the corner for the familiar ginger head—and saw a heap.

Someone had crumpled up and was lying quite still on the stone floor. William dashed across, shouting for Foxy above the noise. They arrived together and found it was Tim.

'Tim, Tim, wake up!'

Foxy tried to lift his head, but it was too late. Badger stood over them roaring, 'Get up, get up! You lazy swine!'

'He's sick. He can't . . .' William began, but Badger turned on him crimson with anger, shouting 'Get back to work, you cheeky pup. You're fined. You're fined. And you too,' he shouted, turning on Foxy. Then, before they could stop him, he kicked Tim in the ribs.

The dinner-bell clanged. As everyone streamed past, Tim moaned, opened his eyes, tried to sit up and collapsed back onto the floor, hair dark with sweat plastered to his white face.

'I know what'll bring him round a treat,' Badger said with his nasty smile. 'Come along then, Uncle Badger will make you better.' Stooping down he scooped up the thin, lanky body, hurried out of the door and across the yard to the river.

'No, no!' Foxy shouted, but Badger had tossed Tim into the cold, racing water. William rushed for the bank but Badger dealt him a back-hander across his face that sent him reeling.

So William had to watch, horrified, with the rest. Now, shuddering with cold, Tim crawled slowly, ever so slowly, towards the river bank. Although William had never exactly liked bossy old Tim, no one would treat their worst enemy like that. How could Badger be so cruel? Though his face still hurt, William rushed forward to help Tim climb out before he could be swept away by the racing current. With Foxy on the other side, they hauled him upright between them and this time Badger did not interfere.

'Woke you up proper, didn't it?' he jeered, but he looked uneasy. Even Badger could see Tim was in no state to work. 'Well, don't stand about gawping! Get him in there!' he shouted, pointing at the sleeping shed.

Tim was no weight to carry. In the shed the two of them stripped off his sodden clothes and rolled him in a blanket.

That night Foxy and William slept on either side of Tim, though there was little they could do for him. Hot as fire to the touch, he tossed and turned for hours, babbling strings of words that made no sense. William could make out only 'Portsmouth' and 'Mother'. But by the morning, Tim was silent and still and cold. William hurried Charlie outside while Foxy went to speak to Crake.

Everyone was very quiet all day. They were too frightened to speak Tim's name, but they all knew that he was dead.

Later, William managed to get Foxy alone for a moment. 'Foxy, we've got to get away from here!' he whispered urgently. His friend had only time to nod before Rob and the others caught up with them. A nod was enough though to cheer him up and set him planning again. Next day, as they were going to bed, Foxy murmured in his ear, 'I've been thinking. We'd best stick it out to the end of the month and get our money.' William wasn't sure he could put up with Dark Hows that long.

A new wagon-load of children arrived during the night. As they went into the mill next morning, William felt a hand on his arm and a plump, rosy girl—one of the new arrivals, you could tell—said, 'Hello, you must be Lucy's brother.'

'Yes, but how did you know?'

The girl laughed. She had not yet learned that no one laughed at Dark Hows.

'Why, you're just like her, aren't you? Straight fair hair and big brown eyes. She said I'd be sure to recognize you. I'm Betty.'

'Is she all right?' William asked anxiously.

Betty pulled a face. 'Well, the workhouse isn't exactly home, is it? Still, she sent you her love—and this.' Quickly she thrust something which felt like a thick folded paper into his hand. William hid it in his jacket before they went into the mill.

A message from Lucy! He'd never expected that. There was no time to look at it until breakfast. Then, gulping down the thin porridge to get that out of the way, he found a corner of the yard and tried to smooth the crumpled paper out flat against the wall. Lucy couldn't write. She had been too little to learn before their mother died, and Father had never got round to teaching her, so perhaps she had got one of the older children to help her.

Then he saw what was on the paper, and shook with laughter. There were drawings of mice all over it—a very large one with black eyes and wild whiskers and seven very small ones. Why, brave Tigermouse must have been a she! And now a proud mother of seven babies! Down at the bottom was scrawled a big shaky letter L and fifteen kisses. How on earth could Lu look after eight mice? But it was wonderful to have her 'letter'. Later, he found himself whistling as he swept. Soon he would be going back to her anyway. He had lapsed into a daydream of the journey home, how they would make for kind Mrs Lane and her jugs of milk, when he was brought back to earth by Foxy dashing over to him, looking quickly round to see if anyone had noticed.

'Quick! Is your broom any longer than mine?'

'Why? What's up?'

'It's . . . it's the doughnut,' Foxy said, shamefaced over such a little thing. 'It fell out of my pocket and it's rolled right into the farthest corner and I can't reach it.' His face was pinched with misery.

William knew this was no ordinary doughnut. It was Foxy's last little bit of home. Thrusting his broom toward him he said urgently, 'Here, take mine and see if—'

'You idle beggar's brat!' roared out Crake, who'd crept up behind them unseen. The terrible iron stick came down with such a whack on William's left arm that he let out a wild yell and doubled up with the pain of it. 'That'll teach you to stand about and gossip in my mill!'

Crake glided away on noiseless feet. Foxy had grabbed the broom and fled back to his pitch. William's left arm hung limp and useless. He felt sick with the pain of it, but somehow managed to stoop and pick up Foxy's broom. If he didn't keep going, Crake would come back and beat him again with the billy-roller.

As he tried the first one-handed shove, pain shot all down his arm. He longed to roll up his shirt sleeve and look at it. Was it broken? Were sharp ends of bone sticking through the skin? No grown-up to turn to for help ... *You have to set broken bones, put them in splints. Father made a pair for our neighbour when he fell off the harbour wall* ... Diving under the machines made William gasp with pain. When at last the bell sounded at eight o'clock and they could rush out into the cool evening air, he was one of the last to leave, fearful of his arm being jostled in the crowd.

Foxy was coming back toward him across the yard, all worried.

'Sorry I let you in for that, mate. I thought Crake was right the other end. Give you a beastly wallop, didn't he, the swine,' Foxy said angrily.

William nodded. 'Did you get the doughnut back, though?'

'Yes, I did. Your broom just reached.' He lowered his voice. 'Just hidden it behind a loose stone in that tumbledown bit. Thanks mate, won't forget that.' Foxy looked white and tired, no longer the jaunty joker of the wagon.

'Look, Foxy,' William whispered. 'We can't wait till the end of the month. One of us could be crippled—or worse,' he added, remembering poor Tim.

'Sunday,' Foxy said quickly, for Badger was herding them into their sleeping quarters and there was no more time to talk.

By the dim candlelight, William eased off his sleeve. The top of his left arm was one enormous dark purple bruise, the size of a duck egg and oozing blood. When he lay down, the pain throbbed all through his body. Tired as he was, there seemed no hope of sleep. Foxy had gone off at once, but Charlie tossed and moaned and murmured about 'hosses'. William sat up in the darkness, holding his hurt arm as if in a sling, and trying to take his mind off the pain by planning their escape.

They couldn't leave Charlie behind, could they? He might slow them down, but if they left him at Dark Hows . . . He remembered how Badger had treated Tim. His mind tried to blot out Tim scrabbling with awful slowness across the rocks.

Next day he and Foxy took their bread and dripping right over to the river bank where no one else cared to go now.

'There's Charlie,' William said.

Foxy nodded, his mouth full. 'Got to take him.'

'Should we slip out last thing at night, Saturday night, d'you reckon?'

Foxy chewed and thought, said finally, 'Badger's going to notice us gone Sunday morning, when we go in to clean the machines, isn't he?'

'Mm. So when shall we—' but Charlie had wandered over to them.

'D'you know, Willum, I heard hosses the other night,' the little boy said eagerly. 'All dark it was but I woke up and I heard clip-clop, quite close, and then I listened a bit longer and it let out a big neigh like it was talking to me.'

'I expect it was bringing the new children,' William said, rolling his eyes at Foxy for all they would now have to leave undecided. They daren't risk Charlie dancing about the yard shouting *I'm going to run away and find the hosses!*

'And Willum, d'you know,' Charlie went on, 'I think it might have been Daisy.'

You couldn't be cross with the little boy: his eyes were all dark-shadowed and his skin looked blue, as if it were stretched too tightly over his bones.

'Yes, maybe it was Daisy,' William said patiently, just as the bell clanged and they had to go back to work.

It seemed that the week would never end. In quick snatches of talk they decided to leave on Sunday whenever there seemed to be a good moment and not to tell Charlie in advance.

William's left arm was still weak and painful, the bruises changing to interesting shades of green. He could waggle his fingers, so nothing was broken, and by Sunday he could even bend his elbow a little.

When they came out of the mill after cleaning the machines, the sun was shining down into the yard and the high hills all around stood green against a clear blue sky. William felt choked with excitement, could hardly gulp the hard bread at dinner-time. He kept his head down in case anyone should notice the excitement blazing from his face. Goodbye to Dark Hows! Goodbye forever!

There was only one way out of the yard, an alley between high stone walls, which they had never had the chance to explore. As usual on Sundays, most of the children were lying half asleep in the sun.

'Go now?' Foxy whispered.

'Why not? Everybody's nodding off and I haven't seen Badger all morning. Presently you wander across to the alley-way and if no one's noticing, disappear.'

'And you'll come after with Charlie?'

William nodded. They looked at each other, eyes shining with glee. William had wanted to tell Foxy about his silver piece, how it would keep them in food for a while, but that could wait. They would follow the sun to the south... As William fingered the

71

treasured coin deep in his pocket, Foxy began to get up. 'Got to get the doughnut,' he murmured, but William nudged him to sit down again.

'Look out, mate, here comes Badger.'

Badger strutted over to them, hands on hips, his fat stomach stuck proudly out in front of him. They saw why: he was actually wearing a waistcoat, like a gentleman. It was a bit darned and stained, but still a bright purple. Anything not faded to grey counted for brand new at Dark Hows.

He loomed over the sleepy children. 'Here, any of you lot got any money hid about you? 'Cos it's against the rules, see. Mr Crake would be very angry indeed if he thought any of you was breaking the rules, you know. Like as not he'd get out his billy-roller, and we don't want that, do we?' he said, with an evil smile.

The dozing children woke up, shook their heads, pulled out empty pockets. Then Badger strolled across to William and Foxy. They looked frantically round, but he had them cornered. 'Here, you with the red thatch, turn out your pockets.'

Slowly, Foxy stood up. 'Haven't got anything, honest.'

But Badger grabbed Foxy's wrists in one great paw and thrust the other swiftly into Foxy's pockets, small eyes gleaming with greed. Finding nothing, he gave Foxy a shove that sent him reeling back against the wall. Not a halfpenny so far: Badger was not having a good harvest.

'Now you,' he said grimly, pointing to William.

6

The Fight with Badger

He shan't stop me—he shan't have my silver piece,
William thought wildly, as the other children froze,
still as rocks, and Badger waited with his evil grin.
With his left arm still painful and weak, there was no
hope of beating Badger in a fight.

William stood up as slowly as he dared, edged
carefully between the others as if going meekly to
turn out his pockets. Very quiet it was, only the river's
sound washing through the silence. Beyond their
group, other children lay about the yard in heaps,
half-pillowed on each other like puppies, too exhausted from the week's work to want anything but
sleep.

'Get on, then. I ain't got all day,' Badger said.

He was just beyond the reach of Badger's arm so he
suddenly dodged sideways and took to his heels,
shooting right across the yard to the narrow alley
between the mill sheds. Shouts behind and pounding
boots. Badger was fat though. He'd would soon get
out of breath, wouldn't he? Down the alley quick!

William burst out of the far end into another smaller yard surrounded by more tall stone buildings. There were two ways out. He tore across the yard and shot along the left hand turn. Badger had seen which way he went, and shouted 'Hey, I want you!' He was so close now, William could hear him panting.

He shan't have my money, he shan't stop me, cried the voice in William's head. *Oh, let this be the way to the road!* Gaining, was he? As William rounded a corner, sure enough the footsteps behind began to slow. He really was winning then. Breath came in great gasps. All the time one hand held the silver piece safe in his pocket. He was nearly out of Dark Hows! Soon he would be heading south, back to Portsmouth and Lucy. Would Foxy somehow grab Charlie and run?

A stitch hurt his side but he went tearing on. He rounded another corner. There was no one about. The pounding boots behind had slowed almost to a walk. That fat bully Badger was giving up!

The last yard was very small, piled high with bits of old spinning machines and broken skips. High walls surrounded it on every side. There was no way out. Desperately William turned back to the alley, but Badger was already strolling into the far end, not hurrying any more, knowing the layout of the buildings, knowing that William was trapped.

Climb the wall—anything— gasped the voice in his head. *Up the rubbish heap*, that would have to be the way. Though his left arm hurt badly now, William sprang up and clutched the end of an old beam with his good hand and swung himself up like a monkey, so that by the time Badger actually entered the yard, he was already halfway up the heap.

Quick! Stretching up as high as he could, his fingers could just scrabble at the topmost stones of the wall. There must be a road on the other side. Then he felt the pile move beneath him as Badger kicked it. *Oh no—must get to Lucy . . . Tigermouse . . .* At last he managed to strain up and hook his fingers over the top of the wall, but at that very moment, Badger aimed another kick at the rickety pile and the whole heap of rubbish gave way beneath him with a great crash so that he rolled down, panting, choked with dust, and fell right at Badger's feet.

The bully was taking no chances this time. He straddled the mouth of the alley-way. He wasn't grinning either. As William struggled to his feet, one hand shot out and grabbed him by the collar while the other plunged into his pocket and snatched out the silver piece. Badger's small black eyes shone with glee at the sight of it.

'Uncle Badger doesn't like little boys who don't do as they're told,' he said softly. 'He doesn't like them at all.'

William wriggled wildly, kicked, grabbed at the greasy black and white hair.

'Give it back! It's not yours, you fat thief!' he shouted, tearing in fury at the purple waistcoat. *My only money in the world, my Portsmouth money.* Then

Badger gave him such a clout that he fell back against the rubbish, knocking his head on a broken plank just as Badger's boots thudded into his ribs, his legs, all his bones. William gasped with pain, frantically trying to roll away, to protect his injured arm.

'Don't reckon you'll run away from Uncle Badger again in a hurry,' the fat boy said at last, grinning down at him. Then he turned away and made off, whistling a tune between his teeth and tossing the precious silver piece in the air so that it flashed brightly in the sunshine.

William lay there, heaving with dreadful sobs of pain and anger, blood trickling down his cheek, dizzy and sick. *Just lie there and die*, he thought. It would hurt too much to move, ever again. *Just lie there . . .* When at last he did open his eyes, the first thing he saw was Lucy's drawing. It had fallen from his pocket in the scuffle and come unfolded so that Tigermouse was grinning straight at him through her whiskers. *Come on, get up*, she seemed to be saying, *this is nothing to a boy who survived the wreck of the* Royal George, *like me*.

So gingerly he sat up, slowly testing arms and legs. His ribs and damaged arm ached horribly and as he managed to stand up, clutching the wall for support, his head went all giddy so that the yard spun round him darkly.

When at last the stones stood still again, he stowed the drawing away in his pocket and began to creep back along the alley-way, to the other turning—the turning where he had made his big mistake. There was no going back to work at Dark Hows now. He could never face Badger again, not even for Foxy and Charlie. He must get away somehow, even if he could only hobble like this. Would that turning show him the way to the outside world?

Down here in the gorge, dusk came early, for the great hills soon shouldered the sun out of the sky. Already the air was turning chill and grey. *Careful*, he must not meet Badger again, not ever. The grey stone buildings of the mill lay still and silent. When he got to the second yard he crept into the right-hand passageway and inched along it with his heart racing, pausing now and then to lean against the wall when the dizziness threatened again.

At last he arrived at the back of the mill, and an open gate onto a track. He walked out. Out of Dark Hows! Turning a corner he found the river running at his feet, the water dark and fast but breaking into white foam where it chased over the rocks. It all seemed so simple. He had walked out. He had left Badger—and Foxy and Charlie—behind.

He would follow the river then. Somewhere it must reach the sea and ships. Would anyone take him on as cabin boy, let him work his passage to Portsmouth? He had no money now, not so much as a penny. What a swine Badger was to steal his silver piece! It could have made such a difference. Besides, he should have been setting out with Foxy and little Charlie, not all alone.

William stumbled along the path, stopping often to peer fearfully back at the looming height of the mill, and leaning against the wet, stony wall of the gorge to get his breath back. Only when the trees came down to the river, blotting out the sight of Dark Hows, did he stop trembling.

He had never been in a wood before. Cold and strange it was, with dusk beginning to fall, very quiet with just the leaves rustling in a small evening breeze, as if the trees were whispering to each other, *look, there's a stranger here*. He wished Foxy was there to crack a joke. His bruises seemed to have joined together in one long ache and the chill, damp air made him shiver.

Then William heard a louder rustling behind him. Oh no, not Badger coming after him again! He blundered on faster through the gathering twilight, his joints beginning to stiffen up now, head whirring like the mill machinery. Or was it the roar of the river? Through it all he could hear footsteps, running behind him, following. Desperately he tried to run faster, but his foot caught in some unseen root and he fell, sprawled on the mossy bank with the whispering trees spinning round him faster and faster as the footsteps came closer and closer and he shut his eyes tight, so as not to see that hateful fat face leering down at him.

'Are you hurt?' asked the river . . . or the trees . . . A gentle voice, anyway. So he had to open his eyes.

There was just enough light to make out two boys,

one tall and one short. They were strangers. But it was a girl bending over him and the end of a dark curl tickled his nose. He sneezed and tried to sit up.

'I—I thought you were someone from Dark Hows,' he stammered, weak with relief. 'You're not, are you?'

'From that hateful place? No, we're not. Are you hurt?' asked the girl worriedly, her finger tracing a dark line of blood down his cheek.

'Had a fight,' he said stoutly. Well, he had tried to fight.

The girl turned away for a moment, murmured to the boys, then turned back to him.

'Look, you'd better come home with us. We're from Clearbrook. They won't mind.'

Anything was better than lying in this cold, spooky wood all night, afraid still that Badger might come after him. So, aching and hungry, he staggered to his feet.

'I—I'm William Brett. Which way is it?' he managed to ask.

'Down along the river,' said the short boy.

That was all right then, away from the mill. He took a step.

'Look out, Rachel!' exclaimed the tall boy, darting forward. 'He's going to fall.'

William toppled into a bottomless pit of whirling darkness.

When he did come to, William thought he must be sleeping still and dreaming, or perhaps he had died and this was the Heaven his mother used to talk about. For he was in a small, whitewashed room, in a small white bed, lit by a white candle. All cosy and comfortable, he lay deep in the hollow of a feather mattress with a smooth sheet against his face and a warm brick wrapped in flannel by his feet.

Stretching carefully, he felt for his bruises, but his body was all cocooned in a flannel nightshirt, just like the one he used to wear at home. *Where am I?* he wondered. There'd been some girl, hadn't there? Couldn't seem to remember . . . His stomach gurgled with emptiness, but the warmth and quiet soon lulled him off to sleep again, until presently he was woken by a gentle hand on his shoulder.

At the sight of a tall, elderly woman in a long white apron, smiling down at him with a bowl of steaming bread and milk in her hands, William struggled stiffly to sit up.

'There's my lovey. Just you eat this up for Miss Emily, then you can drop off to sleep again for as long as you like,' she said.

William slept till five o'clock on Monday afternoon, then most of Tuesday, waking now and then only to eat a bowl of onion soup or brown stew. By Wednesday morning he was beginning to feel better, and meant to ask Miss Emily where he was. It all came back to him now, the plan to run away, the fight with Badger, the lonely wood and some name . . . Rachel, that was it. What had happened to Foxy though? Had he managed to get away as they had planned? Had he taken little Charlie with him? He longed to know, falling once more into sleep.

Next time he woke thinking of Lucy. He was getting stronger. He'd soon be ready to start south. He wondered what she was doing and remembered the story he had started to make up. Where had he got to? Something about a coach at the door of the workhouse, that was it. So... *There was a footman, standing there holding the door open and Lucy climbed up the step into the coach and off it rumbled through the streets of Portsmouth, along the Hard where she could see tall ships sheltering in the harbour, and the sun glinting on the water, making her own private 'magic'.*

Then the coach drove along grand, wide streets until it came to the edge of the country and turned through tall gates into a long drive with trees and grass on either side. It finally came to a halt outside a stone mansion, like the ones they had seen in Oxford, with Lady Harriet waiting, smiling, at the foot of the steps. Lucy alighted very carefully, so as not to trip, and made a curtsey— without falling over. This charmed Lady Harriet and she took Lucy by the hand into the house.

Lucy gazed round with her big brown eyes at all the shining furniture. Father had sometimes worked in big houses like that and told them about the pictures on the walls and the stuffed sofas and chairs. He used to bring home pieces of wood, too, and teach them to name each one by its colour and grain. So Lucy went over to a highly-polished table and asked politely, 'Is this walnut?'

This pleased Lady Harriet no end. 'What a clever girl!' she exclaimed. 'Now you must come and have some lemonade and cake, then I have a surprise for you.' Lucy looked all round for the surprise, but Lady Harriet said it was upstairs.

Sitting down to drink the lemonade, Lucy had to arrange her skirt carefully because of course Tigermouse was sleeping in the little bag slung from her waist and whatever she did, Lady Harriet must not know about her. Lucy knew that such ladies, poor things, were actually scared of mice. When she had finished her delicious cherry cake, Lady Harriet said, 'Come along, Lucy. We'll go upstairs and find your surprise.' Which was . . . which was . . . was . . . William couldn't keep awake any longer on his soft pillow.

Next morning he woke very early. He stretched and for the first time there was no pain at all. When he lifted his head the room stayed still. In fact, he felt just like new! At once he climbed out of the warm nest of bed. By grey dawn light he could see that his shins were turning interesting shades of green and yellow as the purple bruising faded. He was all right. He had escaped from Dark Hows! He could start for the south.

Someone had even put his clothes ready on a chair, all washed and darned. Heigh-ho for Portsmouth then! Should he head directly south, or follow the river to the sea? Quickly, he began to dress.

Suddenly, from outside, there was a sound like hundreds of birds cheeping and rustling and singing together, starlings maybe. Opening the window and leaning out, he could just see dozens of children skipping and hurrying along towards... He leaned out even further until he could just glimpse the corner of a huge stone building which could only be—a mill.

Oh no! Was that all he had escaped to, just another mill? He was about to crawl back under the bedclothes and hide away in despair, when the door opened.

Miss Emily, seeing him dressed, smiled, her face crinkling up.

'Why, you're really better at last then, William. That's my good boy. You're to go and see the Master now, Mr Robins.'

Master! At once he remembered Crake's sharp white face and the terrible billy-roller and his knees began to tremble.

But Mr Robins was different. He sat behind a desk in a room lined with books. They were all the way up and down the walls: William had never seen so many. Mr Robins did not wear a wig like a grand gentleman, though. Instead, his own brown hair was drawn back in a bow of black ribbon from his stern, lined face. His voice, when he told William to sit down, was deep and serious, but kindly.

'Now, William, you were running away from Dark Hows, weren't you?'

'Yes, sir.'

'Tell me why.'

So William blurted out his whole story, from the wreck of the *Royal George* to the death of Tim and the fight with Badger, leaving out only the matter of Tigermouse.

'You won't send me back to Dark Hows, will you, sir? Please, please,' he ended up. 'I'd rather do anything than go back there.'

Mr Robins smiled for the first time, a gentle sort of smile, both stern and friendly.

'Never fear, William. I would never send anyone back to that God-forsaken place. In fact, I should like to destroy it. I must tell you, that man Crake has been to see me already, demanding to know if you'd turned up here. I shall have to pay him some money in compensation,' he went on. 'That is, if you promise to stay at Clearbrook and work for me.' He waited a moment, while William took in this new turn of events, then said, 'It will be quite hard work, but we shall treat you kindly, as one of God's children. I think you know that already.'

It was true. No one had been as kind to William as Miss Emily, not since his mother died, but he had thought he was on his way south . . . Lucy needed him. A picture shone up inside his head of HMS *Victory* sailing out of harbour with all her sails billowing in the breeze. He had to sniff very hard and swallow twice.

'Are you worried about your sister?' Mr Robins asked, his long face anxious again.

'I really had made up my mind to go back to Portsmouth, sir. You see, Lucy's never been without me before, not since our mother died, and now she hasn't got a father either. I promised her I would come back.' Besides, he had had enough of mill work and the journey home was all going to be a great adventure. He might even meet up with Foxy again. Though he did not say this aloud, it was just as if Mr Robins heard him thinking. He put his finger-tips together, stared at them and heaved a deep sigh.

'William, it's nearly two hundred miles to Portsmouth. You would quite likely starve trying to get there, and even if you did arrive, you would have no home, no job, no money. I know only too well what happens to boys in that case. They have to beg or steal just to stay alive. Then they fall into bad company and soon they are in the Devil's clutches and before you know it, they become hardened criminals, ending up in jail. I don't want that for you.'

William hung his head. The man wouldn't help him get home, that was plain. Two hundred miles! His shoes would fall to pieces after the first ten. At last he said, in a very small voice, 'Mr Robins, if I have to promise to stay here, I shall never see Lucy again unless I can earn enough money to save up for the coach fare to Portsmouth.'

'What are you good at, William?'

'I can carve things, sir. I was going to be a carpenter,' and just for a moment his fingers longed to curl round the handle of a chisel. 'I can read and write too. But I'll work at anything you—'

Mr Robins sat back in his chair, his face all bright as if a lantern had been kindled inside it.

'Read and write!' he exclaimed. 'Oh, that will please Elizabeth—my wife, that is. Now listen. I cannot help you directly with money. It's all I can spare to pay off Crake for you, at the moment, because we don't make so much profit as they do at Dark Hows. The children work shorter hours here and we feed them properly. But you won't be fined, so you'll have your weekly wage and a little bit of spare time. If you run errands for Miss Emily, the housekeeper and perhaps help Mr Baines, you could earn a few extra pennies towards your coach fare.'

'Oh yes! I'll do anything.' He had jumped up already, impatient to start. As long as there was hope of getting back to Portsmouth and Lucy sometime, he would work and work and work. 'What does Mr Baines do, please?'

'Ah, Tom Baines is my right-hand man. He's a carpenter by trade, so you'll learn from him. He keeps all our machines in working order. Give him a hand in your spare time.'

'I'd like that,' William said eagerly. 'I can plane and chisel and saw.'

'Then you promise to stay and work for me, William?' Mr Robins asked.

The ship in his head had sailed far out of sight beyond the island.

'I promise,' William replied, head back. 'And— and thank you very much for rescuing me.'

'It was Rachel, Mr Baines' daughter, who did that, and the boys. Off you go then.'

But just as William bolted for the door, Mr Robins called him back. 'Look, I wouldn't go too far up the river on your own if I were you, boy. It's only two miles to Dark Hows, you know.'

7

Ring of Fire

'Race you!' Rachel shouted, brown curls flying, and William bounded up the steep slope between the ash trees, out onto the grassy hillside, up between the outcrops of pale limestone, neck and neck with her, panting and laughing. With a last spurt at the sight of the bramble bushes ahead, he made a quick dash and grabbed the first berry.

'You won,' Rachel sang out, flopping down on the sunny turf. 'You couldn't have beaten me a month ago, William.'

He grinned, flexing his muscles. 'William Brett, strong man of Derbyshire!'

'Come on then, strong man, get going on the bushes. We won't half have to search about today. Most of the blackberries are over.'

It was late October now. At first he had been afraid all the time that Badger would search him out. After all, Crake, his boss, knew where William was. But weeks had gone by with no sign of the bully, and weeks at Clearbrook seemed to fly past. It was still hard work in the mill, but he was a piecer now, dashing from machine to machine joining up broken threads, a responsible job, not so deadly boring and back-breaking as that endless sweeping. The hours were shorter, too, and they sat down at tables to proper hot meals.

He moved along from bush to bush, thinking over the past weeks. Best of all was having his own bed, in a little room with Big Fred, the ten-year-old giant, little Shorty, and Benno, the funny clowny one, his new friends. Big Fred and Shorty were a partnership; Fred had the muscle and Shorty the brains. Benno was an odd, independent boy, always thinking up tricks to amuse the others. No one had quite taken the place of cheerful old Foxy. Still, it was pretty good here, with Sunday free all day.

Big Fred was teaching William to box and Rachel always took him on the expeditions she organized, searching for nuts or mushrooms or kindling wood. Perhaps because she was the carpenter's daughter and motherless, Rachel seemed to have a special friendship with Miss Emily and nearly always got her own way. Of course, they had to walk into Tadwell to church in the morning, but he enjoyed getting out of the mill into the country lanes, and singing hymns, even if he didn't understand all the long words in the prayer book.

There was something very special about Mr and Mrs Robins: they seemed so loving and caring of everyone. Was it being close to God that made them like that? Poor old Tim had said that God was in people, so God must be part of Mr and Mrs Robins, William thought, puzzling it out. He always thought a lot on Sundays. The rest of the day he was free—to pick fruit for Miss Emily, as they were doing now, or do odd jobs of planing and sawing for Mr Baines. It was a treat to feel a plane in his hands again and find he had not forgotten how to use it. Mr Baines was a silent man with wonderfully clever hands. He hadn't wanted to trust William with a chisel to begin with. Now, in his quiet way, he seemed glad of his offers of help and would slip him a penny now and then, so that all the time his small hoard of money was growing. Every wages day brought him nearer to Lucy.

As William reached across to the next bush, Rachel suddenly appeared, barring his way, fingers purple, face unusually stern.

'Let's go back,' she said urgently. 'Now, quick. Let's find the boys.'

'Why, what's the matter?' William asked. 'We haven't got anywhere near enough yet.'

'We've gone further along this way than we've ever done before. Come on back!' and she snatched at his arm. Ever since bringing him back to Clearwater, Rachel had adopted him, but he wasn't going to be bossed about by a mere girl, even if she was Mr Baines' daughter. Dodging sideways, he made for the next bush—and skidded to a halt. A golden autumn sun was setting now behind the western hills, but that was not the reason for the cold creeping up his spine, a cold that made him shiver. No, they had never come this far before. Far down in the valley below, where the ash woods thinned out, he could see a huge, looming shape. Dark Hows!

Earlier in the week, there had been a rumour about a local mill being burned down. Mr Robins said that some of the cottagers who had always spun at home hated the new mills which took away their jobs and made them send their children out to work. William had hoped so much that Dark Hows had gone up in smoke, as long as the children escaped. But there it stood, whole and solid. Even Mr Robins had called it 'that God-forsaken place'.

Without a word, he turned back. Soon they were slithering down between the ash trees, yellow leaves drifting past them through the darkening air, until Rachel grabbed at a tree to check her speed.

'Will,' she whispered. 'There's someone down there, look, on the river path.'

'It'll be Fred, or Benno. They said they'd see us on the way back.'

'It's none of our boys,' Rachel replied.

He peered down between the smooth grey trunks. Gazing up at them was a fat white face beneath dark hair streaked with white. Badger!

'Come on, let's climb up again,' William hissed, his right leg, the one Badger had kicked the worst, giving a stab of pain as it still did sometimes when he was tired.

'No good, he's seen us.' Sure enough, Badger was beginning to climb up towards them, smirking to himself. 'Will, climb that tree,' Rachel said into his ear.

'No, no, I can't leave you to face—'

'It's not me he's after, is it? Quick, get up there,' and she slid away into the dusk.

Badger's oily voice shouted up at him, 'Why, there's naughty little William who ran away from his Uncle Badger. Come along now, there's a good boy. Uncle Badger's come specially to take you back to Dark Hows. Mr Crake will be ever so pleased to see you again, won't he now? Probably have a special welcome!'

The sound of Badger's voice made William feel sick, the pain jabbing in his leg to remind him of Badger's terrible boots. He shinned up the nearest tree and had reached a fork about twelve feet up by the time Badger appeared directly below, panting and angry from the climb. William had never let himself think much about the death of Tim, but it was suddenly clear now that really Badger had killed him, by throwing him in the cold river when he was so ill already. So it was a murderer down there...

When Badger got his breath back, he grabbed the slender trunk of the ash and began to shake it violently so that William had to cling on with all his might. As Rachel must have guessed, Badger made no attempt to climb up. The thin tree would have snapped under his flabby weight. Even shaking it seemed to tire him quickly.

'Stay up in yer nest then, poor little frightened

bird,' Badger jeered. 'Old Badger will wait for you. You see, Mr Crake doesn't like little boys who sneak off to another mill, not when he's paid for them, oh no, he doesn't like that at all. He's probably got his old iron stick all ready and waiting for you. D'you remember his special stick, little billy-roller?'

Now it was William's left arm that twitched at the horrible memory. He thought of the dirty blanket on the hard stone floor. He wouldn't go back, not ever. Did Badger really mean to wait down there all evening—all night? He wouldn't be able to cling on all that time. In the end he would fall down there among the ash keys right beside Badger's dreaded boots, murderer's boots. What if Badger meant not to take him back to the mill at all, but to kill him out of revenge for his escape? He daren't speak now, in case his voice shook and gave him away, but Badger rambled on, enjoying himself.

'I've been looking for you, you know, oh yes. Mr Crake's going to be generous, you see, very generous, when I get back with his little lost lamb what he was so fond of. A very nice green coat for Sundays, velvet an' all, I understand.' Then as William kept silent, he grew impatient again, jumped up, gave the tree another violent shake, his voice changing from its self-satisfied purr to a rough shout. 'Come on down, you little rat. You know I've got you trapped up there!'

William clung on for dear life. The good food and sleep of Clearbrook meant that he was much stronger now, but not strong enough to fight Badger. Big Fred and the other boys must have gone home long ago. His right leg was hurting horribly, squashed against the fork of the tree, and his shoulders felt as if they were on fire with the effort of holding on, just like that time on the mast of the *Royal George*. The whole world seemed to be shaking.

'You're making your old friend Badger rather cross, you know? In fact, very cross indeed. And there's no knowing what Badger might do when he gets really cross!' He sounded deadly dangerous. The wood had grown quite dark and silent except for the rustling of the trees. 'Think how pleased little Charlie will be to see you again,' Badger went on. 'Poor little boy, misses his friend, don't eat much. Don't suppose he'll last much longer.'

Charlie! Badger knew how to hurt all right. All these weeks at Clearbrook, William had tried to forget the other place, had vaguely hoped that Charlie had got away with Foxy, or was being looked after by that girl, Jill.

'Charlie!' he exclaimed, and lost his concentration just for a second. He slipped and all but fell headlong, clinging on with one hand while he scrabbled wildly for a foothold on the smooth bark as Badger sniggered below.

'Don't be afraid. Uncle Badger will catch you.' He was laughing aloud now. 'And take you home to little Charlie. I dare say he might last a few more days if you was there to cheer him up, poor little skeleton.'

Charlie and his 'hosses'. How could he have let himself forget? The shock of the little boy's name might well have destroyed William's chance of staying in the tree, for his new perch was desperately precarious. He would fall soon, he knew, gazing fearfully down at the white streak of hair that showed up through the darkness. There would be no one to see what happened then . . . But, just as the tree began to shake again, William saw a light flare up behind Badger, then another to the left and yet another, further round.

'Hey, what's going on?' Badger shouted, as he, too, saw the lights. 'Who are you?'

There was no reply. The lights came steadily nearer, yet moving round all the time so that you could not tell how many there were. Badger stopped shouting and made a dash for freedom, but he was ringed in now by the circling torches, their leaping flames shining on his fat white face as it broke out into a sweat of fear. William half-climbed, half-fell out of the tree, sliding behind the nearest torch-bearer, Big Fred.

With a quick grin he handed William a spare torch, a cudgel of wood with a knot of tarred rags at one end, lighting it from his own as they continued to circle Badger. Then a voice William recognized as Shorty's called out, 'What shall we do with Badger?' and another, Benno's, cried, 'Yes, what shall we do with Badger, eh?'

'Throw him in the river!' Yellow flames danced on

yellow leaves and shadows leapt wildly about the wood. When Badger tried to shove his way out of the moving circle a torch was waved in his face so that he jumped back with a yelp of fright.

'Beat him!'

'Burn him!' mocked his invisible tormentors round the weaving circle. Badger jumped clumsily to the other side, but again, flames beat him back. At his third try, a blackened face ringed with flame, like a demon from hell, was thrust into his. That was the end. Badger's stocky knees gave out entirely at the sight of Benno's terrifying features and he fell in a fat heap among the autumn leaves, pleading with them, 'Let me go. Let me go! I didn't mean any harm. I was only teasing.'

At first William had pranced round laughing at Badger's downfall. Now he felt almost sorry for the terrified flabby youth grovelling there at his feet. Slowly the circle wound down, came to a halt and William realized there were only three others, his room-gang.

'If you ever come near William or Clearbrook again,' Big Fred said quietly, 'we shall do all the things we promised, Badger. Now clear off and don't ever come back.'

Badger stared dumbly at the four of them, staggered to his feet and slunk off into the darkness between the trees.

'I say, Fred, you just about saved my—' William tried to thank his friends, but already they had set off back, leaping and whooping down through the wood, so he ran with them and their leaping shadows, stretching his cramped limbs, free again.

'Whoo-hoo, whoo-hoo!' echoed round the rocky gorge, so that the pigeons woke in their tree-top roosts and clapped their wings in annoyance. Soon their dying torch flares gleamed on the river's racing black water and they were home at Clearbrook with Rachel coming to meet them.

'Rachel, you were marvellous, fetching the gang so quickly. Why, you must have run all—' but once again William's thanks were interrupted, for just as they were dousing their torches in the yard tank, Miss Emily came hurrying towards them calling out, 'William, you bad boy, out in the dark!' She sounded more worried than angry. 'I've been looking everywhere for you. You're to go and see Mrs Robins at once. She's waiting for you.'

'*Mrs* Robins?' he asked, surprised.

'That's what I said. Wash yourself quickly now and go up to the Master's house.' Miss Emily even forgot to ask where the blackberries were, which was just as well, since they had left them behind.

The terrace of cottages where William lived with the others, Apprentice Row, stood high on a bank above the yard, facing the mill, with the river on the right and the winding lane to Tadwell on the left. William hurriedly washed his hands and face. For a moment, clean and tidy now, he stood in the middle of the dark yard, looking round him.

Candlelight glowed from the windows of his row. Somewhere a girl was singing. Soon it would be Sunday supper-time, thick brown stew and dumplings, then apples from the orchard. He had earned a halfpenny for picking them up. Afterwards they would go on sitting round the long tables singing hymns with Mr Robins until bedtime. Running back through the woods just now, he had actually thought of Clearbrook as 'home'. How could two mills be so different?

The thought of Dark Hows made him remember Charlie and the things Badger had said. Something about 'a skeleton' and 'last a few more days'. Of course he might have been exaggerating, but it sounded only too horribly likely. William felt ashamed for having forgotten the little boy while he revelled in nice food and a comfortable bed. Perhaps he could tell Mrs Robins about Charlie?

Whatever can she want? he wondered, climbing the steps to the big house. *Surely I haven't done anything really bad?* He wasn't scared of Mrs Robins in the way he was scared of say, Crake, but all the children respected her, and never played around when it was their turn for reading.

Every afternoon some of the children had lessons in the dining-room. The younger ones went three times a week, the older ones twice. William mostly did arithmetic because he had never really learned it before. Well, he had known enough to measure wood, but not seven eights are fifty-six or five thousand six hundred and eighty-seven divided by nine. Rotten old sums! But he worked hard because it might help him get a better job later on, Mrs Robins said, setting him awful long divisions which crawled right down his slate.

A very serious lady she was, but pretty, even a bit like his mother when she did smile. Her fair hair was drawn back in a simple knot and she was so slim round the middle in her silky dresses that Rachel declared she daren't laugh much or she'd snap in half!

She was not smiling at all when William was shown to her sitting-room by the maid. He had meant to start at once and tell her about Charlie, but she looked at him so gravely and said, 'William, where have you been so late? I've been dreadfully worried about you.' So he tried to cheer her up and began straight away telling her about Badger and the rescue, doing his best to make it into a funny story.

But at the end she only looked graver than ever and said, 'Badger was a wicked boy to treat you like that. But we must pray for him, William. God has changed worse people than Badger.'

'Yes, Mrs Robins,' he said uncertainly.

'I wish we could have him here . . .' she continued quietly. William shuddered. She seemed to be talking to herself. 'If he could know that God loves him . . .' Then she turned back to William and said sternly, 'Don't go near Dark Hows again, child, not anywhere near. You won't always have Rachel to come to your rescue. And that youth, Badger, is going to hate you and Clearbrook more than ever now, don't you see?'

Then she began to cheer up a bit, patted a stool by the fire for him, smiling. 'But that isn't why I wanted to see you, William. Sit down. I am very pleased with your lessons. Now, there are so many little ones who cannot read at all, I simply can't find time for everybody myself, so I want you to help me teach them, for half an hour, every Monday and Thursday afternoon. Would you like that?'

He stared into her gentle blue eyes, unable to believe it. A teacher!

'Oh yes—yes. Well, I—I mean, if I'm really good enough. What—what will the other chaps think, though?' he stammered out. Most of them were friendly enough, but some of them still looked upon him as an outsider, that boy from Dark Hows.

'I'm going to ask Shorty and Rachel too, so you won't be the only one,' replied Mrs Robins.

William felt ten feet tall. 'Thank you! Thank you very much, Mrs Robins.'

'And, William, teachers get paid, you know.' Her eyes were twinkling now. She must know about the Portsmouth fund, he thought. 'At least a halfpenny a lesson, I should think.'

Another penny a week nearer Lucy, he thought, springing down the steps three at a time. The yard was half-lit by the cottage windows and in the mill itself a lantern glowed where Mr Baines was mending the frame of a machine, ready for tomorrow. Only towards the river lay deep darkness and a chill mist rising. It was all very well his dancing for joy because life was so good here. Further up the gorge Charlie would sleep hungry and miserable on a cold floor. He had never managed to tell Mrs Robins about Charlie, and really, she had enough to worry about with all the children here. He would have to do something himself.

He would have to go back to Dark Hows and rescue Charlie.

8
The Raid

'Then the goblin said . . .' William looked round at the others' intent faces lit by the dim, candle-stub light. As usual, Benno was telling the story. Every Sunday, when they were sent to bed early, they had a story-telling session. Benno was very good at acting it all out, his dark face lively, black eyes flashing, hands waving. Sometimes he even capered about. But William didn't really like his stories. They were full of witches and demons and death.

'And that was the end of the goblin,' Benno finished up.

Big Fred shook his head slowly. 'That was a real good'un. I don't know how you make all that up,' he marvelled.

William said quickly, before Benno could begin again. 'I've got a story now—a true one. It's called Charlie and the hosses.'

'Oh good,' Shorty said with a grin, settling down again. 'I like true ones.'

'Well, once upon a time, that is about the end of

August,' William began, 'there was this little boy living with his grandfather at an inn.' He went on to tell them all about Charlie being put on the wagon at Portsmouth and how he made friends with all the horses, how he had hidden between Georgina's great hooves and how he had finally come to Dark Hows.

'He'd like our Montague, wouldn't he?' Big Fred said. Montague was the big brown and white dapple who delivered supplies from the village twice a week.

'But that's not the end.' William went on to tell them what Badger had said, how Charlie was only a skeleton, might not last much longer. It made him feel quite choked, saying it aloud.

There was silence for a moment when he finished.

'Poor little squit,' Big Fred said at last.

Shorty's usually friendly blue eyes had gone hard and serious.

'Something... something ought to be done,' he murmured, talking to himself. William held his breath. He knew the idea of a rescue must come from the others. 'Something...' Shorty looked round at them. 'We can't just leave him there to die, can we?'

Benno had his eyes shut, not pleased that someone else had told a good story, but Big Fred said, 'How could we ever get him out of that place?' With his rumpled fair hair and puzzled frown, he looked like a worried retriever dog. At that moment the candle flame sputtered and died.

'Night then,' Benno murmured, half asleep already. So no more was said, but William curled up in his bed with a secret, gleeful grin. He had got the gang interested in rescuing Charlie.

By Monday bedtime they had all worked too hard to want anything but sleep. On Tuesday William had to take his first reading lesson, with a little thin boy called Billy.

'A is for apple,' William said, drawing a big A on his slate. 'Now you copy that and say, A is for—'

'I likes apples,' Billy interrupted, 'big red juicy ones that—'

'Yes, all right. Copy the A. Right. Now, B is for butter,' William went on. 'Write a big letter B and say B is for—'

'I loves butter,' Billy cried. 'All yellow and squishy. I like it spread real thick on a girt slice of new bread, and then some—'

'Draw letter B,' William said again, patiently, not finding teaching quite as easy as he had expected.

When they were going to bed that night, Benno said, 'How's teacher then?' in his mocking way.

'I had to teach a skinny little chap called Billy, who looked a bit like Charlie,' William said swiftly, glad of a chance to mention him.

'I've been thinking,' Big Fred said, slowly.

'We've been thinking, you mean,' Shorty interrupted. 'We've sort of thought of a plan, how to rescue Charlie and bring him back here. But it all depends on you, Benno.' William admired Shorty's cleverness. He knew just how to persuade their spiky, independent friend.

Benno was already lying down in bed but snapped upright, important again. 'Yes, yes, what d'you want me to do?'

'William, what time do they go into the mill on Sundays? That's the only time they work when we don't, isn't it?' Shorty asked.

'Before six o'clock.'

So they laid their plans. They would creep out in the middle of Saturday night, get to Dark Hows, snatch Charlie and bring him back to Clearbrook where he would be found wandering around as if lost. William was especially worried about the last bit. It seemed only too likely that Charlie would blurt out, 'Willum fetched me', but he had to risk it.

As the week went slowly on, they talked through the plan at every bedtime, adding more detail each time.

At the next reading lesson, William got his pupil as far as F.

'F is for frog. Here's F. Now you copy that and write a big F on—'

'I hates frogs!' Billy cried. 'They's all slippy and slidey and they hops all over you and they—'

'Billy, write letter F,' William said firmly.

In spite of Billy's interruptions, Mrs Robins seemed pleased with the lessons and gave William a penny, putting an arm round his shoulders and giving him a little hug. 'Thank you very much,

William,' she said, just as if he were a grown-up. 'I will see you again on Tuesday.'

William went thoughtfully down the steps of the big house. Sunday came before his next lesson. Of course he was pleased they were going to rescue Charlie and thought how Miss Emily would put him in the little goosefeather bed and feed him up with chicken broth until he was strong and lively again. But the plan itself worried him, seemed too full of things that might go wrong. Over it all hung the shadow of Dark Hows. He had sworn never to go near the nightmare place again, and here he was, faced with walking right into the heart of it.

A robin whistled as he crossed the yard back to the mill: winter was coming, but it was not the cold that made him shiver.

However hard he worked, scurrying between the rumbling, clacking machines, catching the flying, broken threads, Friday seemed to last for ever. On Saturday the four of them were on tenterhooks all day, for the sky was overcast, clouds hanging low in dark rolls like old feather-beds. Their plan would only work if it were moonlight. Even then it would be hard enough to find their way up through the ash woods.

As usual on Saturday evening at Clearbrook, the whizzing overhead power belts slowed to a halt, the big wooden frames stopped lumbering to and fro on their iron wheels and the bobbins stopped whirring round. The machines were closed down early, so that they could be cleaned, ready for Monday morning. They had to be cleaned, otherwise they would clog up with all the soft, drifting filaments of cotton and grind to a halt at the wrong time.

When the boys came out of the mill at supper-time, the clouds were beginning to shred away. When they went up to bed, Benno stuck his head out of the window and exclaimed, 'The stars are out. Hurray!' Now that he had an important part to play, Benno was mad keen on the raid.

William was to stay awake till midnight, then wake Shorty for the next shift. They could just make out the gilt hands of the mill clock, shining faintly in the starlight. They planned leaving at five in order to reach Dark Hows at six, when the children would start to cross the yard to the mill to clean the machines.

William did not lie down for fear of nodding off to sleep. Dark Hows ... suppose Badger appeared, just as he had grabbed Charlie, or Crake got up early for once with his iron stick? Then there was Charlie himself. At the first sight of his friend, wasn't he going to shout, 'Willum, Willum!' and tell the whole world?

William tried to think of something else, awake alone. Fred was snoring already. Lucy. Lucy would be fast asleep too, wouldn't she, fair hair spread all over the pillow. What was that story he had been telling himself about her? She was in Lady Harriet's grand house, wasn't she? Yes, that's right... *Going up the stairs to a big bedroom with shiny curtains and one of those strange beds like the one Father once had to repair, with tall posts at each corner and curtains all round, so you could shut yourself in. Lucy stood and stared and Lady Harriet said, 'Come and see what I have for you, dear.'* Lucy ... Lucy ... With a sigh he gave up. It was no good, he couldn't really escape into Lucy's world, not tonight.

At five the next morning Benno, doing the third shift as they had arranged, woke William and the others. They crept down the cottage stairs, shoes in hand, climbed out of the dining-room, collected their stuff from a corner of the yard and set off along the river path. It had all gone without a hitch.

The old moon hung deep yellow in the sky, netting their feet with moving leaf shadows. The black river rushed past on their right, foam gleaming where it broke over rocks. The fallen leaves beneath their feet gave off a bitter, earthy smell, like beetroot.

'We've done it!' Benno exclaimed, once they were a safe distance from Clearbrook. He threw the two unlit torch sticks he carried with him into the air and juggled with them.

'Mm. Best keep quiet though,' Big Fred whispered, steady and calm. William was glad he would have Fred with him at Dark Hows, but he felt sick, just the same. Suppose ... Then a pigeon flew up from the high branches, clapping its wings, making them jump. They fell about, sniggering and snorting with suppressed laughter, bumping into each other.

'Sh! Must be nearly at the bridge,' Fred said quietly. They threaded along the edge of the bank, stepping from moonlight to shade to moonlight, confused by the shifting shadows, a chill wind sighing in the branches overhead.

'There it is!' Shorty exclaimed, pointing.

The bridge had been made when the trunk of a large tree had fallen slap across the river long ago. Its top was now worn smooth. Benno leapt lightly up onto it and skipped across, vanishing into the darkness on the other side, but Shorty looked askance at the racing water just below and climbed slowly up onto the trunk on all fours.

William had never liked this part of the plan. Benno and Shorty were to walk up the far bank until they were opposite Dark Hows. As soon as they heard the children coming out and crossing the yard, they were to light their torches and dance about and juggle with them to create a diversion. This would turn all eyes away from the sleeping quarters while William and Fred grabbed Charlie—who was always one of the last to get up.

As Shorty hesitated on the bridge, Benno reappeared, flickering in and out of the fading moonlight, running back across the bridge. 'Come on,' he whispered to Shorty, taking his hand. 'It's easy as pie. Blackberry pie!' Together they crossed over and were soon out of sight.

William heaved a sigh. It was all up to him now. Could he find the right way through that warren of stone alley-ways from the road to the inner yard? As they padded on up river, the moon was going down westward, the colour of old cheese, so that there was even less light, but their eyes had grown accustomed to the night and there were still the stars. He wasn't half glad of Big Fred, so large and friendly beside him, as the ash trees whispered together in the darkness, and unknown creatures rustled about, close by, at home in their night world.

Then Fred stopped him with a hand on his arm, pointing ahead. The trees fell away, but up ahead a great blackness blotted out the stars—the roof of Dark Hows. Up till now William had felt ashamed of his fright and the way his knees kept trembling. But the actual sight of the place he dreaded so much caught him up in a wild mood of daring. He would dash into the yard, grab Charlie, whisk him back to Clearbrook and in no time at all, Miss Emily would have him right as rain, working in the mill and he would be able to give him reading lessons. H is for hosses!

'Come on, round the back,' he whispered to Fred, with a grin.

Had Benno and Shorty managed to make their way along the opposite bank? They didn't really know if there was a path that side. It was very dark now, under the looming walls. As he edged slowly along so as not to make a betraying sound, William could hear his heart going thump-thump with excitement. It was so quiet no one could be up yet—good, they had timed it well. William put out a hand to feel where the wall turned a right angle—and at that moment a terrible deep baying broke out just in front of them as a great black shape with glaring eyes hurtled round the corner, straight at them.

William leapt sideways as the huge dog sprang at him, felt a rush of hot, meaty breath as it knocked him aside and threw itself at Fred. There was a muffled cry of anguish, a choked voice hissing, 'Run, run!' and shouts now from behind the walls, thudding footsteps, furious barking.

Suddenly William was running, galloping back along the dark path by the river, more scared than he had ever been in his life, with Big Fred beside him. He tripped and fell, but Fred dragged him to his feet and they tore on, past the bridge, breath coming in loud gasps, until Fred stumbled to a halt and they stood listening.

William could hear the deep barking still, but it was in the distance, not coming any closer.

'Did he get you?' he asked anxiously.

'Got my arm,' Big Fred said. 'Hurts something awful.'

'He must have been tethered there, or he'd have come right after us.'

They trailed miserably back along the river, the darkness greying towards dawn, pausing now and then to listen.

'D'you reckon Benno and Shorty will realize what happened, and come back?' William asked presently, but Big Fred only grunted, cradling his right arm with his left.

Then they heard footsteps, quite close behind them. William pushed Fred up the bank, into the shadow of the trees, peering fearfully down toward the path, wishing it were still dark night. It turned out to be Benno and Shorty.

'We heard all the hullabaloo and thought we'd better come back,' Shorty said, as they met up. 'We were scared you'd been caught.'

'Fred's hurt,' William said. 'The dog got him.'

They peered at Fred's arm, realized the sleeve of his jacket was dark with blood.

'What shall we do?' asked Benno. 'It's been no fun so far.'

'Fred's got to have help with that arm,' Shorty said firmly.

'We'll take him to Miss Emily. She'll know what to do,' William said.

It was daylight when they trudged into Clearbrook yard. Blood was dripping from Fred's sleeve now and the big boy looked very white. William dashed off. It was all his fault: he even remembered now, too late, that he had heard the barking of some large dog that very first night at Dark Hows, when he couldn't sleep. He found Miss Emily in her starched white apron, stirring porridge by the kitchen stove.

'Miss Emily, could you come a minute?' he said urgently. 'Big Fred's been hurt.'

'Oh deary me—and what sort of a hurt would that

be?' she asked, placidly going on stirring, used to their frequent bumps and bruises.

'It's a dog bite, and it's bleeding a lot. Could you come now?'

She came then at once, took one look at Fred and led him away without a word. He didn't come to breakfast. William couldn't eat his porridge. Shorty and Benno didn't speak. The three of them made a small pool of silence in the cheerful Sunday hubbub. William knew the whole story of the raid was going to come out.

After breakfast they had their usual wash and smarten up, then lined up in the yard in twos to walk to Tadwell church. Shorty and Benno went together and the rest with their friends, Rachel with her father. William usually walked with Benno, but today he tagged along on his own at the back, not wanting to talk to anyone.

In the golden autumn sunshine, the woods along the lanes glowed amber and bronze and yellow; birds flew up, startled from gobbling bright berries and a breeze bowled little puffs of white cloud across a high blue sky. But William saw none of it. The raid was all his fault. It had been a stupid plan, he could see that now. He longed to see Fred and find out how bad his arm really was. Suppose . . . suppose he were to lose it . . .

They trooped into the small stone church where the sun, shining through tall pointed windows made coloured patterns on the floor. *Please, God, make Fred better*, William tried to pray. When the white-haired clergyman, Mr Gregg-Thomas, climbed up into the pulpit and gave out some chapter and verse, William's brain blanked it out, kept swerving back to that dreadful moment when the great hound had sprung from the darkness. By day it must have been kennelled somewhere among the stone alley-ways at the back of the mill and at night tethered by the roadway in case of intruders—or anyone trying to escape. He remembered now, in that hubbub of voices at Dark Hows, one had been shouting, 'Bruiser, Bruiser!' And the dog was kept secret, though Badger would know about it. Probably it belonged to Crake.

Please, God, rescue Charlie, please!

Shorty must have thought he was falling asleep, for he gave William a sharp dig in the ribs, recalling him suddenly to the church, where the sermon was just coming to an end.

'And so I say to you, my friends, let us not flinch from this hard task. Make it your chief aim this week and in the weeks to come to throw away every thought of hatred, and forgive your enemies as did our Lord.'

Clergymen were supposed to be clever, William thought, shuffling to his feet as the sermon ended. How could Mr Gregg-Thomas go on like that, expecting him to forgive Badger for stealing his silver piece, beating him up, coming after him, throwing Tim in the river? Even Big Fred's arm was his fault really.

Almost as soon as they were back at the mill,

sitting about the sunny yard waiting for the dinner-bell, Rachel ran across to him.

'William, Mr Robins wants you, up at the house,' she said. William swallowed twice, marching up the steps. He had only wanted to rescue his friend. What was so bad about that? Let Mr Robins rant and rave—see if he cared. He had done it for Charlie. He stalked into the book-lined study white-faced but defiant.

Mr Robins sat at his desk writing, his long face stern and grave. For a while he went on writing, eventually laying down his quill pen and looking up at William. Even then it was a long time before he spoke. At last, very quietly and sadly, he said, 'We trusted you, William. We took you in and made you better and trusted you. How could you go and do this sly, underhand thing? Mrs Robins is so upset.'

This was far worse than any ranting and raving. William wished he would shout or even give him a beating, either would have been easier to bear. He didn't know what to say. In the end he muttered, 'It was because of what Badger said, sir, about Charlie not lasting much longer . . .'

'You only had to come and tell me about little Charlie and I would have tried to help him,' Mr Robins was saying. 'But you couldn't trust me. You had to go behind my back and lead other boys into danger.' William hung his head.

Mr Robins gazed out of the window and seemed to be talking to himself. 'Elizabeth and I have tried so hard to make Clearbrook a Christian place,' he murmured, disheartened. 'A place without fear and lying and cruelty. As for Charlie, well, we shall have to see . . .' He turned back to William, sighed, and said, as if he were very tired, 'Go away, boy. Go away.'

William wanted to blurt out that Clearbrook *was* a wonderful Christian place and ask about Big Fred's arm, but it wasn't possible. He slunk out, feeling about an inch high. The rest were having Sunday dinner, brown stew and dumplings, but he didn't feel like eating. He wandered off into the deserted orchard, curled up in a sunny corner under the wall, tired after his almost sleepless night and the walk to Tadwell.

Nobody here cared about him or Charlie. Lucy would care. He wondered what she did on Sundays, far away in Portsmouth. A wasp droned past his ear. Shutting his eyes he tried to blot out the world of the mill and think about Lucy, to lose himself in that story he had been dreaming up about her. Where had he left her last time? Upstairs, that's right, in Lady Harriet's bedroom.

'I have a surprise for you,' Lady Harriet said, and there on the bed was a little dress, just Lucy's size, of blue silk. Lucy put out a finger and touched it and when the silk rippled, it shone like the light on the sea and Lucy exclaimed, 'It's magic, magic!' Lady Harriet did not understand what that meant, but she was pleased that Lucy liked it and said, 'Try it on, dear.' Now Lucy was torn two ways. It was the most beautiful dress she had ever seen and she was wild to try it on, but if she took off her old smock Lady Harriet would see the bag with

Tigermouse in it and probably throw her straight out of the house.

For a moment Lucy stared at the 'magic' dress, then she said politely, 'Please, Lady Harriet, it's rude to undress in front of people, isn't it?'

Lady Harriet thought this was comic, coming from such a little girl, but she laughed and said, 'All right, I will leave you to change,' so Lucy stripped off her shabby brown smock and . . . and . . .

When William woke, the sun had gone from his corner. He felt all cold and stiff. After jumping up and down a bit to get warm, he went in search of Miss Emily, finding her by the kitchen stove, darning socks.

'Please, Miss Emily, how is Fred's arm?' he asked.

Slowly she wove her needle through the frayed strands, then she looked at him sadly and said, 'His arm is very sore, poor lamb, very sore indeed.'

That night, Fred's bed was empty. No one felt like telling stories—even Benno was very quiet. Next day, when they flocked out of the mill at dinner-time, Montague, the big brown and white dappled horse, was standing in the yard, tossing his head with a jingle of harness as the week's supplies were unloaded from his wagon. Charlie would have been over there, feeding him titbits, William thought miserably. Everybody seemed to have forgotten Charlie. The only thing to look forward to was his reading lesson with Billy on Tuesday. Perhaps he could get him as far as K for king and Mrs Robins would be pleased.

But when he went across to the big house on Tuesday afternoon, Mrs Robins was waiting for him at the top of the steps, looking as if she might burst into tears at any moment.

'I shall not be needing you today, William,' she said. 'Or Friday,' and she turned away quickly, drawing a lace handkerchief from her cuff as she went back indoors.

William was stunned. This was worse than any other punishment. Would she ever let him be a teacher again? The only good thing that day was Big Fred appearing at supper, his right arm swathed in bandages. Shorty cut his food up so that he could eat left-handed with a spoon.

When they were going to bed, William asked, 'How is your arm, Fred?'

'Miss Emily's put a comfrey poultice on it, but it's all purple and horrible and swollen,' Fred said.

Benno stared at William and said, 'Didn't you know about the dog?'

'No—not really.'

'How could you live there all those weeks and not know about it, then?' Shorty demanded.

'It—it must have been kept hidden away somewhere,' William said lamely.

'Fred could have been killed if the dog had got his throat,' Shorty said accusingly.

'We'd never have gone if we'd known about the dog,' Benno said.

After that, no one spoke. William ached with

weariness, but could not sleep. Everyone hated him then. Even gentle Mrs Robins had turned him away. If only he had cheerful old Foxy to talk to . . . Lucy still loved him though . . . He couldn't stay here with no one to talk to. He'd go back to Lucy.

He would run away, back to Portsmouth.

9

The Enemy Strikes

William slipped away from supper early on Monday evening to count his money. Outside, a chill grey November fog settled over the hill as the ash trees lost the last of their yellow leaves. Not good travelling weather, he thought glumly. Strewn across his bed the coins looked ever such a lot. A long time ago, when he first came to Dark Hows, he had asked Mr Baines how much he thought the coach fare would be to Portsmouth. The carpenter had scratched his head, said he didn't know exactly, but he reckoned it might be a couple of guineas or more.

When William counted up all the halfpennies and pennies and sixpences, they only came to four shillings and ninepence halfpenny. Not even five shillings, and it took twenty-one to make a guinea! He would have to walk the two hundred miles to Portsmouth then, eking out the money to buy food on the way.

William had wondered if there was any way he could get Charlie to come with him, but the great dog meant he dare not go to Dark Hows again by night and daytime seemed equally impossible. Anyway, the prospects of getting home again safe and sound looked rather bleak. It wouldn't be fair to involve Charlie in such a risky expedition.

William decided he would leave next Sunday night, as soon as the rest of the boys were asleep. That meant he would get one more week's wages and wouldn't be tired after a day's work, so he could set out and walk all night.

The next week seemed an endless round of work, food and sleep. No one was angry with him any more, but his secret plan cut him off from the others now. Sunday came at last. In the evening, Mr Robins told them Bible stories, about Jesus feeding the five thousand, and another about him changing water into wine, then they sang hymns round the long table as usual and when they had finished, Mr Robins said cheerfully, 'Well now, next week we must start practising carols for Christmas.'

William wondered sadly where he would be next Sunday, when they were all singing the lovely old tunes round the table. Suddenly Benno struck up: 'Oh come all ye faithful, Co-o-ome to be-ed,' and, as they scraped back the benches and made for the stairs, everyone took up the tune and went off singing, while Mrs Robins stood watching them, her fair hair shining in the lamplight, smiling gently at their high spirits.

'God bless you all and sleep well!' Mr Robins called up after them.

Benno didn't offer to tell any stories that evening. Shorty helped Big Fred undress because his arm was still padded up with bandages. William took his clothes off so as not to rouse any suspicions. Soon Fred was snoring and the other two seemed fast asleep, so he slid out of bed and dressed again by feeling about in the dark. He stowed his money deep in a pocket, tucked his shoes under one arm and was ready.

Tiptoeing over to the window, he stood there looking down into the dark yard. The fog had cleared away now, revealing a sky brilliant with stars. Good, so it wasn't going to rain. Out into the lane and turn left, as usual, for Tadwell. Near the church there was a milestone which said fifteen miles to Derby and after that he must follow the sun. He knew the way then, at least to begin with, but still didn't move from the window.

He tried to raise some excitement, to think how thrilled Lucy would be to see him again, but he could only remember how Rachel had rescued him twice, how Miss Emily had nursed him up in the goose-feather bed, how Mrs Robins had hugged him . . .

Was that someone moving, down in the blackness of the yard?

A voice in his head was saying coldly, *They've been good to you, haven't they, all the people at Clearbrook, and you let them down, hurt Mrs Robins badly. It was your fault about the dog too. You should have remembered that barking on the first night. And you've never even said you were sorry . . .*

There *was* someone down in the yard. All was dark in the mill. Mr Baines sometimes worked late on Sunday nights so that the machines could start up in good order first thing on Monday morning, but William knew he had finished early because he had come to join in the hymn singing. Peering down, he caught sight of a squarish, bulky figure that seemed horribly familiar.

Couldn't really be Badger, could it, down there, under his window? He would have to go and see, even though the very thought made him shiver all over. Then, suddenly, inside the great building, he glimpsed a flickering light—flames!

'Shorty, Shorty, wake up!' he shouted, shaking his shoulder.

'Eh, what?' murmured Shorty sleepily.

'Shorty, wake up! There's a fire. Wake the others, quick, and everybody!'

Dashing out of the door and along the passage he banged on every door as he galloped past, yelling, 'Fire, fire, wake up! The mill's on fire! Help, help!' as he tore down the stairs and out into the yard.

Oh. Was it all a mistake? The mill wall rose up in front of him like a black cliff against the stars. There was no light anywhere. He wouldn't half look a fool for waking everybody up ... but then he smelled smoke, ran round the corner—and gasped.

The ground floor of the furthest wing of the mill was alight, every window lit by a dull red roaring glow. *Get in somehow? Back door?* As he shot past one window a tongue of yellow flame burst out of it, as if to suck him in. The next window was smaller and lower—the office. Staring in, he could see by the red glare a thin body fallen across the threshold of the far door into the mill proper.

Mr Robins—in there! Already the coiling black smoke was making William cough. Shouts behind him meant that everybody was waking up, but they would be too late to save the Master. Coughing and hot, he ran back into the yard and plunged straight in to the water tank to wet his clothes, to stop them catching fire. The shock of cold made him gasp and choke more than ever, but he jumped out again at once, grabbed the buckets always left ready by the tank, filled two to the brim and staggered off back to the fire.

Figures appeared out of the night, shouting, jostling for more buckets. A voice was calling, 'Over here, boys, make a chain.' Good, that was Mr Baines. He would know what to do. 'Pass the buckets along to me and the next boy run back with the empty one,' he was shouting.

When William lifted the latch of the office door, it burned his fingers, but he opened it. Foul, choking smoke swirled everywhere, getting up his nose, into his lungs, making his eyes stream with tears. Through the doorway he could see the limp body of Mr Robins only too well because by now the doorway itself was on fire.

'Mr Robins—Mr Robins!' he cried out, but the Master never moved. The heat was growing more fearsome all the time.

Picking up one of his buckets, he threw the water over the doorway, dousing the flames on one side long enough for him to slip through. The fire was leaping over the whole office now, licking towards him with a terrible roaring sound. William heaved up the other bucket and spilled the water all over Mr Robins. Still he didn't move, so William caught him round the middle and began to drag him backwards towards the door.

Where were the others? *Oh come on somebody, help, help, never get him out in time! So heavy...* As William panted and struggled, the smoke choking him, and vicious flames roaring toward him in a great red wave, clouds of even blacker smoke from the burning cotton store threatened to blind him.

Never do it, never! He staggered backwards, sick and dizzy, feeling the weight of the Master dragging him down and down, until suddenly a blast of cold air meant that he was at the door. Then he was through it and outside in the chill, sweet night air, gulping it like water.

He laid Mr Robins well away from the fire, on the grass. Was he dead? Behind him, every boy and girl was passing buckets up from the river to try and save the cotton store and he ran towards them by the light of the flames shouting, 'The Master—he's here—he's hurt. Get Mrs Robins, get her quick. He's—'

A shout went up all round the yard, as they began to understand. 'Mrs Robins! Mrs Robins!'

A girl brushed past William, long fair hair flying out above a black cloak. Only when she threw herself down by the Master did he realize it was Mrs Robins with her hair streaming loose. By the yellow fire-flicker he watched her grave face as she thrust a hand inside his shirt.

'He's alive! He's alive, William!' she exclaimed. 'Here, help me.'

Between them they carried the Master past the sweating bucket chain, across the yard and up the steps to the big house, while behind them the fire began to die down at last. As they laid the limp body on a sofa, Mrs Robins said urgently, 'Fetch Miss Emily, William, quick as you can. She'll know what to do. And William—thank you.'

Now the excitement was over he felt sick and cold inside, though parts of him seemed to be on fire. He tottered back across the yard knowing there was one thing he had to do fast. Everyone was still busy damping down, so no one noticed him slip into the cottage and upstairs. With burned, shaking hands he stripped off his clothes and pulled on his night-shirt. Now he looked the same as everyone else so no awkward questions could be asked.

While Mr Baines stayed in the mill in case the fire started up again, Miss Emily told them all to wash, then come in for hot soup. Still dazed and smarting, William found himself sitting down at the long table with Benno and Shorty and Big Fred—a funny sight they were in their black-streaked nightshirts.

'Hey, look at William!' Benno exclaimed. Everyone did, and roared with laughter.

'It's your hair, mate,' Shorty said.

When William put a hand up to his head, a crisp brown sausage of hair came away, all singed.

'It was you gave the alarm, woke us all up, didn't you?' Big Fred said.

'William, you saved the mill!' Rachel cried, from further down the table, leaning forward, eyes shining.

Monday whirled past. They were allowed to sleep on till eight o'clock, so it seemed as if work had hardly started before it was dinner-time. Miss Emily rubbed burdock ointment onto William's scorched hands and told him Mr Robins was beginning to get better. Some boys asked him for locks of scorched hair. William basked in glory, grinning to himself. No one thought to ask why he had been looking out of the window in the middle of the night. At this moment he might have been trudging south from Derby . . .

Halfway through Tuesday dinner-time, Rachel bustled up to him and said, 'William, Mr Robins wants you at the house.'

He gulped down the rest of his jam tart—it was too good to leave, even for a summons like that.

Mr Robins was sitting up in bed, his hands bandaged, but managing to smile.

'Now William, sit down and tell me all about the night of the fire and exactly what you saw, please.' William told him what he had seen.

'This man you saw in the yard,' continued Mr Robins, 'you didn't actually recognize him?'

'No, not really,' William said slowly. 'I did reckon it might have been Badger, from Dark Hows. He was the right shape.'

Mr Robins nodded. 'You see, when Mr Baines was raking over the ashes, he found traces of tar and candles, so someone deliberately started that fire. It was no accident.'

'They hate you at Dark Hows because you're known to be a kind Master and children want to get away to Clearbrook,' William blurted out. 'And Badger hates me specially, because I did get away. I know it wasn't Crake, because he's tall and thin. Besides, he'd most likely send someone else to do his dirty work.'

'And you're all right, William? You didn't get burned too badly?'

'Only lost my hair, sir, and my hands are still a bit sore. I jumped in the water tank, you see, before I—'

'You are a very brave boy,' said a gentle voice behind him. Mrs Robins had come rustling in. 'You saved my dear husband's life and I can never thank you enough for that. You see, someone had hit him over the head from behind. He would never have come round in time to escape the fire on his own.'

'Got a great bump here,' Mr Robins said, gingerly feeling the back of his head. 'Must have taken someone by surprise, but I can't remember a thing about it.'

William felt himself blush all over. Wriggling, he murmured something about 'glad Mr Robins was better'. They must never know how nearly he had run away! 'We would like to do something for you,' said Mr Robins. 'You certainly saved my life and you pretty well saved the mill as well by giving the alarm so quickly. Thank goodness it's only the office and the cotton store that are badly damaged.'

'It was a real Christian act, William, risking your life to save someone else. I'm very proud of you,' Mrs Robins said softly, making him feel even worse.

'What can we do for you as a reward then, William?' the Master asked.

William was struck all of a heap, didn't know what in the world to say, stared from Mr Robins, stern and kind in his bandages, to pretty Mrs Robins, both waiting for him to speak. Reward! He'd always thought of the word as a heap of gold. Could it mean Lucy, Portsmouth, Charlie?

After a long silence, Mrs Robins said, 'William, I know you love Portsmouth and your sister. Do you want to go back there?' *Yes, oh yes, to Lucy and the shining harbour where the tall ships glided and Tiger-mouse and the Cabin and the feel of a chisel in my hand.* 'But you haven't got a home there any more, or even a job,' she went on, just as if she had heard him thinking.

He blinked. The tall ships had seemed so real for a moment, their sails spread white in the sunshine. Of course, there was no Cabin now, no bunks, no Father singing 'Blow the man down, me boys'. And he didn't even have any tools.

'What would you do, William, if you did go back?' Mr Robins asked.

He remembered the beggar children, plucking at sleeves, whining for farthings, and the boys who flung themselves down in stinking harbour mud while well-dressed visitors threw pennies and laughed at their antics. He had never worked it out in words before, but he realized clearly for the first time why Clearbrook was so different from Dark Hows. It was because Mr and Mrs Robins were Christian people who loved God and tried to show his love to others. His mother had loved God too, so this was where his mother would have wanted Lucy to be. He did care about little Charlie, but Lucy had to come first. Looking up at the Master in his high bed, he said, 'I'd rather Lucy came here, sir.'

Mrs Robins' serious face lit up. She so far forgot herself as to give him a quick hug and exclaimed, 'Dear William, that's just what I hoped you would say. We'll arrange it all. It will take a little while, but perhaps we might have her here for Christmas.' William couldn't speak for joy. 'You see, she'll have to come on the coach as she's on her own, and we'll need to find some lady travelling from Portsmouth who'll look after her. Won't we, my dear?' she said, turning to her husband.

Mr Robins nodded, lying back against the pillows very tired and white. It didn't seem quite the moment to ask if Tigermouse could come as well.

William tore back through the yard. 'Lucy's coming!' he shouted to a startled blackbird. 'Lucy's coming!' he shouted to the thrumming machines, and they roared back.

Two Sundays later, by which time Lucy's arrival was all arranged, William and Rachel went out into the woods after dinner to pick up firewood for Miss Emily. Though every day brought Lucy closer, it seemed an awful long wait.

William and Rachel were perched on a favourite rock by the river, the sun making pale, lacy patterns through bare branches and shining on the racing brown water below. Lucy would love that—she'd call it her 'magic', thought William.

'It's still three whole weeks to the day when I meet the coach,' William said out loud. 'I don't really think she can have kept Tigermouse all that time, do you?'

'She might. She does sound quite a character, your sister,' Rachel said.

'You will help me look after her, won't you? It'll be all strange to her.'

Rachel tossed back her long brown curls with a grin. 'She can be my little sister—she'll have to behave herself, mind! Tell you what, let's make a mouse cage, just in case Tigermouse does arrive.'

'Maybe if we could find a dead tree, I could saw it up,' William said doubtfully, wondering how big a mouse cage needed to be.

'No need for that. Father would let you have enough little bits to build a mouse cage and lend you some tools,' Rachel said, her face bright and eager. 'Don't forget, you're still the hero of the mill.'

'D'you really think he would?'

'Of course. We can make it next Sunday.'

'But then, if she doesn't bring Tigermouse...' William thought aloud.

'Silly, we can always catch her a new one in the mill and call it—Lionmouse.'

'Elephantmouse!'

'Milly the Mill-Mouse!'

They fell about laughing, until Rachel jumped up. 'Come on, we'll never get enough kindling for Miss Emily at this rate. The sun will be gone below the hill.'

November days closed in early and already shadows were beginning to gather. As they turned to climb up the slope, there was a sudden rustle in the bushes above them, as if some heavy animal were moving away. William's heart went thud-thud-thud and footsteps went pounding off through the trees.

'Quick!' William shouted, diving toward the thicket with Rachel close behind, but whoever it was had had too much of a start. They could not see properly through the close trunks of the ash trees.

'Listen!' Rachel whispered.

They heard only the rustling of dead leaves, a pigeon clapping its wings in alarm, then silence. Whoever it was had not run far, was hiding up where it was darkest, in some clump of bushes.

'Badger, I reckon,' William said quietly.

'Did you see him?'

'Not really, but it was someone hefty. He must have been hiding, listening to us talking about Lucy coming for Christmas,' he said anxiously. 'Come on, let's go back.'

'Oh, cheer up!' Rachel cried. 'Who's afraid of silly old Badger, anyway? Race you home. Don't forget it's pea soup and apple pudding tonight.'

No 'magic' light shone on the racing river now. As shadows began to gather in the darkening wood, William began to wonder. Was it right, after all, to bring Lucy here, only two miles from the dangers of Dark Hows?

10
Surprise!

A thread snapped and William leapt across to join it again, expertly dodging the rolling iron wheels and the thrumming overhead belts which channelled the river's power to the machines. He hardly noticed the sweat running down his face or the dusty air making him cough.

'Lucy's coming! Lucy's coming today!' he sang inside himself. Her small white bed was already made up next to Rachel's and, though Miss Emily didn't know, there was a little wooden cage underneath, complete with hollow wheel for an energetic mouse to spin round.

His fingers were usually clever with the threads, but today they fumbled with excitement. The clock above the mill entrance had surely struck one ages ago and he was to leave at half past, walk into Tadwell and meet Lucy's coach. They would be together for Christmas and always. Christmas was going to be a whole day off and roast goose and singing carols round a big bonfire in the yard.

Just for a cold moment he wondered what Christmas would be like at Dark Hows. There'd be no goose and stuffing for Charlie, he was sure. Nothing more had been said about him: everyone seemed to have forgotten the little boy, even God hadn't listened . . .

Snap! He ran down the aisle toward the flying end of cotton. A broken thread held up production, so you had to be as quick as you could. He rounded the corner—and came face to face with a small, white-faced figure with blood streaming from his temple. Shorty, renowned for his speed as a piecer, or joiner-up of broken threads, had tried to dodge one machine too many.

'Shorty! Hey, lean on me,' he exclaimed, for the boy had begun to sway on his feet. He looked wildly round. Fred was sweeping a distant corner, Benno and Rachel were nowhere in sight. He could not see Mr Wavell, the overseer, anywhere. He daren't ask anyone else for help. Even at Clearbrook you could be fined for stopping work. Putting an arm round Shorty, he half-dragged, half-carried him out of the mill.

The thin white boy reminded him painfully of Charlie. A great dark bruise was spreading across his forehead and he had gone quite limp and still. William couldn't free a hand, so he kicked the cottage door until Miss Emily wrenched it open, prepared to be angry. But at the sight of Shorty, she exclaimed, 'Oh, the poor wee lamb. Take him straight up to your room and I'll get water and a bandage.'

William managed to haul Shorty up the stairs and lay him on his bed.

'Miss Emily, he'll be all right, won't he?' he asked anxiously.

'Oh Lord bless us, he'll be fine. He's just knocked out cold for a bit. A dab of my special witch-hazel and I'll bandage him up like a wounded soldier back from the Frenchies. He'll be right as rain in an hour or two,' Miss Emily said comfortingly.

'But he hasn't woken up!'

'He will soon enough, though he'll have a nasty headache, I daresay. Draw the shutters across, child, so he can rest in the dark.'

William went to the window. Stretching up his hand to the shutters, he saw the big mill clock opposite: it said ten minutes to two.

'Lucy! I've got to go,' he cried, bolting out of the room and down the stairs. He was twenty minutes late! *Oh Shorty, why did you have to get hurt, today of all days?* He shot through the yard and out into the lane, panting already. Nearly five to. He had twenty minutes—he'd never do it.

The lane twisted and turned up a steep hill out of the river valley. Soon he was puffing so much he had to slow to a walk. Where the ash trees met overhead, the winter rains had left deep ruts full of sticky mud. At last he burst out of the woods onto bare, sunny uplands where black-faced sheep grazed among outcrops of white rock. He didn't need the sun, he was hot as midsummer, but the brilliant light did

136

make him feel better.

After all, Shorty was going to wake up and Lucy was coming and in five days they would be celebrating Christmas together. He and Rachel had planned it all. They had built her a tree-house in the nearest big ash, for her Christmas present. This morning Rachel had muttered something about another surprise, but he couldn't be wondering about that now.

As the path flattened out, he was able to break into a trot again.

'Lucy, I'm coming,' he panted out loud to the annoyance of a blackbird who flapped off the stone wall in alarm. After all, the coach could easily be a few minutes late, so he might still be there outside the Green Dragon as it came into sight. She'd be sure to be hanging half out of the coach window. That was how he had imagined it, through the weeks of waiting. Even if it did come in right on time, she would only have to wait a minute or two, for he could see the roofs of Tadwell now.

When William swung into the cobbled square, it was empty. No coach stood outside the Green Dragon, its regular stopping place. The clock on the church tower said twenty past two. He was only five minutes late, then, and the coach must be even later, or there would be people about. Oh marvellous ... He leaned against the wall of the inn, content to get his breath back and wait for Lucy. Idly, he watched two horsemen ride by, elegant in their velvet coats, perhaps from the mansion of Chatsworth, not far away, that Rachel had told him about. When the clock struck the half hour, he walked through the archway of the inn, to the stable yard.

'Coach is late today, then,' he said to a boy mucking out a stall.

'No 'tisn't, 'twas early,' said the boy shortly, raking up dirty straw.

'You mean—it's been and gone!' William exclaimed.

'S'right.'

William ran back into the village street and looked wildly up and down it. The only person in sight was an old woman coming out of the bakehouse. Lucy had not come, then? He went all cold inside. Perhaps because she hadn't seen him there waiting for her, she had gone on to the next stop—wherever that might be. She could be miles away by now ... Dashing back to the stables, he asked the boy. 'You didn't see a little fair girl get off the coach, by herself, did you?'

'S'right.' The boy went on sweeping, not interested.

'She did come, then. Do you know where she went?' William cried, frantic now, taking a precious penny from his pocket and holding it out. The boy grabbed it.

'Went off with a big fat chap—heard him say he was sent to meet her.'

'Did he—did he have a white streak in his hair?' William asked fearfully.

'S'right.'

Badger! Badger had kidnapped Lucy! Already

William was tearing along the village street toward the path down to the river, the path to Dark Hows. Because that was where he was taking her, wasn't it, back to that God-forsaken place, to sleep on a stone floor, sentenced to work till she dropped from exhaustion. Maybe evil-eyed Crake would be after her with the dreadful iron stick, or Badger himself might throw her in the river as he had poor Tim.

The path sloped steeply downhill under the trees, slippery with wet leaves. Twice he fell headlong in the mud, but floundered on as fast as he dared. Should he call out or would that make Badger hurry on even faster? The bully wouldn't be able to make Lucy's short legs walk very fast. She couldn't be used to walking far at all.

Now he was down on the gloomy path right beside the racing brown river, could see a fair way along it. No sign of anyone. The sun never reached down into this deepest stretch of the gorge. Dark Hows! Why had he ever asked for Lucy to come to this dangerous place? At least she had been safe in the Portsmouth workhouse... He tried to run faster now that the ground was flat.

He suddenly remembered that Sunday when he and Rachel had sat on the rock, talking about Lucy's arrival and planning the cage for Tigermouse. Then they had heard someone blundering away. It *must* have been Badger, hiding there, listening, learning which day she was coming. He rounded another bend, breath coming in rasping gasps, but still no one came into sight. Suppose Badger had not gone this way, meant to do something even worse with Lucy than take her back to Dark Hows? *Badger will hate you more than ever now*, Mrs Robins had said, after that time when they had chased him with torches. Surely even Badger couldn't hate a harmless little thing like Lucy? Besides, what could be worse than Dark Hows? He skidded to a halt. Where else could they have gone?

He listened, hearing only the river rushing and babbling over the rocks below. Then, after a moment, something else, far distant, but a voice, high-pitched as a bird's. He'd know that voice anywhere. He shot off along the path again, peering ahead through the tree shadows, rounding another bend—and there they were, two hundred yards ahead.

Without thinking he let out a ringing cry. 'Lucy!'

At once Badger broke into a lumbering run, trying to drag Lucy by the hand, but she had turned her head and seen him, was calling, 'William, William!' squeaking with excitement, struggling against Badger to make him stop, slowing him down so that he could hear her crying, 'But it's William I tell you. It's my own brother William. Oh stop, stop, please stop!'

William hadn't had time to think what he was going to do when he caught up with them. The thought came to him now, cold and clear as the river. He had always run *away* from Badger before, never toward him, like this.

'William!' Lucy's little face was all rosy from

hurrying, glowing out from under the old brown hood of a cloak which was now too short for her. 'Stop, you're hurting me!' she yelled, trying to drag her hand away. And Badger stopped. As William came panting up, he swung Lucy into his arms and turned to meet him, a grin on his fat white face.

'You put my sister down!' William shouted.

'Skinny little thing, ain't she? Won't last long at Dark Hows, I shouldn't think,' Badger said gloatingly, licking his thick lips.

'Put her down.'

Lucy stared from one to the other, puzzled as to what was going on. William was in no hurry now, wanted time to get his breath back. For in a minute, he would have to fight Badger. There was no other way. It was as if all his life had led up to this moment.

'Put my sister down and come and fight clean,' he said quietly.

Badger only laughed. 'Oh, she's no weight. Should be a nice nimble little thing. Mr Crake'll love to see her skipping about between the machines. Daresay there might be a new coat in it for me.'

William realized poor Lucy was quite in the dark as to what had happened.

'Look Lu, this boy came and snatched you away. I didn't send him or know he was coming. He's trying to take you and sell you to the wrong mill, where I was first of all—and it's a dreadful place,' he tried to explain as quickly as he could.

'Put me down!' Lucy squealed.

'What, a dear little thing like you?' Badger jeered, putting up his free hand to pinch her chin.

That was his mistake. William had almost forgotten what a temper Lucy had when roused, and now that she knew Badger was an enemy, it was roused with a vengeance. Big brown eyes hot with rage, she seized Badger's ears, one in each hand, and appeared to be tearing them off, till he let out a howl of pain, so loud it echoed from the rocks above, and dropped her.

William burst out laughing, but there was no time to enjoy Lucy's triumph. He squared up to Badger, who seemed to loom over him, huge and angry. As he lunged forward, William dodged sideways, landing a blow on the bully-boy's shoulder that swung him round. Suddenly William found he was not afraid any more. Good food and hard work had toughened him up no end, and in friendly sparring bouts with Big Fred he had learned how to use his feet. Badger might be large, but he was flabby and clumsy too. He soon stopped grinning as William danced round him, ducking and swerving away from his big fists, getting in a sly blow when he could.

'Oh look out, Will!' Lucy was screaming with excitement, jigging up and down. 'Go on, hit him harder.'

He had Badger right on the river bank. The big boy swung a right-hander to William's jaw and as he slipped aside he was only just in time to dodge a left-hander to his stomach, which would have winded him silly. Trust Badger not to fight fair! As Badger's fists met only air, he was thrown off balance. He tried to stagger forwards and William landed a blow on his chin. Badger reeled sideways, flailed the air wildly with both arms, then fell right over backwards, face blank with surprise, until he hit the water with a huge splash.

'Hooray!' Lucy shouted, running over to the bank. 'Is he drownded?'

'It's not deep enough for that.'

Sure enough the black head with its white streak was already breaking the surface.

'Shall we push him under again?' Lucy suggested helpfully.

'No, no. That's enough.' As Badger scrabbled for a hold on the rocks, William couldn't help remembering Tim's thin white hands doing the same. Badger deserved a ducking, but he wasn't a terrifying enemy any more, just a fat, frightened boy floundering in the fast current of icy water, frantically babbling something about 'can't swim'. William had never believed you could really forgive your enemies, but now he asked himself, *what would Mr Robins do?* And he did really feel sorry for Badger, blubbing and choking in the river. The months at Clearwater had made him realize how much better it was to love than hate.

'Jump on him, Will, jump on him!' Lucy was shouting, dancing with rage.

'No, Lu. We've got to help now,' he said, surprised at himself.

Every time Badger tried to scrabble up the slippery

rocks, he fell back, tears streaming down his fat face. William watched him for another moment, then he knelt down on the bank and stretched out a hand. Badger grabbed it at once, hauled himself from the water and scrambled up the bank to collapse in a sodden, shivering heap.

'Shall I kick him again?' Lucy asked, but William was remembering what Mrs Robins had said, how she wished Badger could come to the mill.

Badger at Clearbrook would ruin everything. Badger in the same place as Lucy! He wasn't just a horrible sneering bully, he had really killed Tim and probably meant to finish off Mr Robins by leaving him to die in the fire.

'Come on, quick,' he said to Lucy, hurrying her away along the path.

'Will, I came in a big coach, with a nice lady called...'

So they were together at last, but while Lucy babbled on about her journey and all its excitements, William was not happy. After a few minutes he stopped and looked back. Badger still lay in a miserable heap on the bank. If Jesus could change water into wine, Jesus and Mrs Baines could change Badger into someone better. Without a word, he turned and began to walk back.

'Will, Will, what are you doing?' Lucy cried.

In a moment they were standing over Badger again. 'Badger,' he said slowly. 'You can come home with us. It's good at Clearbrook. The people are kind and they care for you. You'd have a bed and nice food and maybe make friends . . .'

Badger rubbed water out of his eyes and stared up at him in disbelief, mouth trembling. A deep struggle seemed to be taking place inside him, but at last he got to his feet, muttered, 'Shouldn't be anybody there,' and shambled off, along the path to Dark Hows.

William heaved an enormous sigh of relief. Well, he'd tried, and no one would ever know how hard it had been.

'Oh Lu, I don't think he'll ever come after you or me again, now he knows I can beat him,' William exclaimed, with a huge feeling of relief. 'How are you then, eh?' At last he was free to pick her up in the big, big hug he had looked forward to for so long.

'Ooh, don't squeeze too tight!' Lucy cried, throwing her arms round his neck. 'Isn't this lovely, William? I did miss you something horrible. You were ever so clever to arrange for me coming here and all. D'you know,' she paused and studied him carefully. 'D'you know, you look sort of grown-upper.'

'So do you.' He set her down on a rock by the river.

'Do I really?' She preened herself for a moment, smoothing her hair. Lucy had wanted to be 'a lady' ever since she was three.

'Look Lu, you'll never go off with a stranger again, will you? Promise?' William said.

'Course I won't. But he said you had sent him because you had to work. How was I to know he was a lying old bully?' Lucy said indignantly.

He gave her another hug. 'I wish he—'

'Oh, never mind about him any more, Will. We're together again and that's all that matters. There's so much to tell you, it could take years. Besides, I've got a surprise for you.' Big brown eyes shining with glee, she looked carefully round for spies, then plunging a hand down the neck of her skimpy old dress, drew out a red flannel bag on a string necklace. 'You'll never guess who I've brought with me,' she whispered.

'Never,' William whispered back, solemnly.

She loosened the strings, opened the mouth of the bag a little way and held it out to him. Two small black eyes peered sleepily around at the big world.

'Why, it's never—it's not really—you can't have brought—Tigermouse herself!' he exclaimed.

'I have! I did lose her a few times, but she always came back in the end.'

'Well, you clever old thing.' William put one finger in the bag, and a very pointed grey nose sniffed it over, whiskers wildly whiffling.

'There, she remembers you,' Lucy said happily. 'I knew she would.' As he felt the warmth of the little furry body, he wondered if this could really be that same gallant swimmer he had rescued from the wreck of the *Royal George.* He did hope she was. For a moment, it all came back to him vividly, the terrible sinking ship dragging him down under cold green waves... Snapping his mind back to the present, William asked, 'Did you ever go to that

Lady Harriet's house, Lu?'

She stared at him in surprise. 'Why no. Nobody ever went anywhere grand like that. She did come into the kitchen once and patted me and asked if I was being a good girl, or something stupid.'

William laughed. 'D'you know, I made up a story about you going to this great mansion and Lady Harriet giving you a blue silk dress. It all seemed so real.'

'Blue silk dress! I wish she had given me one. I'll tell you what did happen, though. A boy called Foxy, with red hair, came to see me not long ago and brought me a pork pie and said I was to let you know he was all right and working in a baker's,' Lucy said, the words tumbling out.

'Foxy! He did get away then. Well done old Foxy, back with his doughnuts.' William was pleased to hear about his friend. 'And I'll tell you some news, Lu. It's too late today, it'll be dark soon, but tomorrow, if the sun's shining, there'll be 'magic' on the river.'

'Fancy you remembering my magic,' Lucy said. 'Oh Will . . .' and she gave him another hug.

'Come on, it's getting twilight. We'd better get back. Besides, Rachel, my friend, said something about a surprise for us.'

'I love surprises! I keep having them today,' Lucy said happily, skipping along at his side.

Soon the mill came in sight. It was very quiet. There was no one about.

'Look Lucy, there's Clearbrook, through the trees. Miss Emily's the housekeeper and Rachel's going to be your big sister—' he broke off as they rounded the corner of the big house and came in sight of the yard. In the dusk he could just see that it was crowded with people.

A shout went up, 'Here's Lucy! Lucy!' and torches began to flare. William thought he ought to find the Robins. Suddenly, there was Mrs Robins on the steps of the big house. So, pushing through the crowd, he reached her side.

'This is my sister, Lucy, Mrs Robins.'

'Hello, my dear. Welcome to Clearbrook,' Mrs Robins said with one of her rare smiles. Lucy was too overcome with shyness to speak, but she seized the skirts of her threadbare old smock and managed a deep curtsey without falling over.

'Look! Someone else has come to welcome you,' Mrs Robins said, pointing across the yard. In the middle of the crowd was Montague, the carrier's big, dappled horse who seemed to be clopping slowly toward them. What a funny surprise to arrange for Lucy, William thought for a moment, till he came closer and he saw by the flickering torchlight the tiny figure perched on its back, wild with excitement.

'Look Willum, look! I's on a hossie—a girt big hossie!' Charlie cried.

'Charlie!' William could hardly believe it. He looked quickly round. Mr Robins had joined his wife now. William ran over to them.

'Charlie! You've brought Charlie!'

'We wanted to save him as much as you did, William,' Mrs Robins said. 'He's already eaten two bowls of Miss Emily's brown stew!' Still William could hardly believe it.

'But is he here for always? Not just for today?' he asked.

'We managed to get another little bed into your room,' Mr Robins said. A big grin spread over William's face. God had listened to his prayers after all!

Then Mr Baines came out of the crowd. 'Reckon there's room for two up there,' he said, swinging Lucy up onto Montague's wide back and handing William the bridle.

So the dear Robins had rescued Charlie, not forgotten him. *I really should have trusted them*, William thought. Now, proudly, he held the bridle and led the big horse all round the yard with Fred beside him, while Rachel and Benno and Shorty, now quite recovered, whooped around them waving their torches and everyone clapped and cheered as wild shadows leapt up and down the walls of the mill.

Mr and Mrs Robins stood smiling on the steps of the big house, while Charlie just squealed with the excitement of it all and Lucy nearly fell off Montague's back in an effort to wave graciously with both hands at once.

Never mind the sun shining on the river, this was a 'magic' moment, William thought, struck dumb with the wonder of it, but managing to wave to Mrs Robins. He did just have a fleeting wish that Badger could have been there too, to share all the warmth and fun. Perhaps some day, even he would come home to Clearbrook.

11

Goodnight

When Lucy was lifted down from Montague's back at the end of the parade, Miss Emily exclaimed, 'That child looks proper peaky. She'd better come with me.'

Lucy did look white and tired all of a sudden after her long and exciting day. William settled her by the kitchen fire so that she could have a bowl of brown stew from the big pot, then Miss Emily said, 'You'd best take her up to Rachel's room now and see her straight to bed.'

'Did you remember a box for Tigermouse?' Lucy whispered as they went upstairs.

'No, I didn't.'

She stopped abruptly, brown eyes wide with dismay. 'But what will she do?'

'Tell you what,' William said cheerfully as they came into a room crowded with beds. 'We'll shut the door tight and let her have a run. I'll watch her while you get undressed.'

'All right.' She sounded doubtful, but drew out the

bag, put it on the floor and opened its neck. Tigermouse poked her head out, whiffled her silver whiskers and shot off into the darkest corner, beady-eyed, eager to explore a new world.

William brought the candle closer when Lucy was sitting up in bed, and reaching underneath it, brought out the wooden cage he had made and set it on her lap.

'This is for Tigermouse. I thought she would like it better than an old box.'

Lucy squeaked with surprise. 'Will, Will! A proper cage! She'll love that.' Then she turned on him, punching his shoulder with both small fists. 'You was teasing me!'

He gave her a quick hug. It was wonderful to have Lu back, to tease. He sprinkled some bread crumbs inside the cage and showed her how to bolt it with a wooden crosspiece.

'It's got a wheel!' she exclaimed, peering inside.

'Yes, that's for exercise.'

He was very proud of the cage with all its intricate dovetailed joints and smooth bars. Using carpenter's tools again had filled him with a deep, secret joy.

'Quick, let's put her in.'

Tigermouse had skittered all round the room, keeping close to the wall, but she was very tame and easily caught. For a moment she sat on the palm of his hand outside the open cage door, then lifted her long nose, smelled the breadcrumbs and nipped inside. She didn't eat at once, but sniffed about suspiciously while Lucy held her breath. When she put a paw on the wheel, it started to spin and she jumped back.

'She'll get used to it soon,' William said, stowing the cage away under the bed. 'Time you were asleep.'

'I don't feel so sleepy now.' Lucy stared round the strange room.

'That's Rachel's bed. She's going to be your big sister,' said William proudly.

'I had a friend, Marion, in Portsmouth,' Lucy said. 'One of the big girls. She took me down to the harbour to put me on the coach. And there it all was, the shiny water and little boats and one big ship sailing out and the air all fishy and seaweedy and . . . and . . .'

'And you wanted to stay?' he asked gently.

'Only if you were there too,' she said loyally. 'I'd sort of forgotten it a little bit. There was the alley-way up to Mrs Brown's and the Cabin.' She was quiet for a moment. 'D'you think we'll ever go back there, Will?' she asked, brown eyes wide and wistful.

'Of course we shall,' William said, surprising himself.

A plan had been forming in his head over the last weeks. It had all begun with making the cage for Tigermouse.

Lucy sat bolt upright, her fair hair shining in the candlelight. 'But it's an awful long way, Will. I thought we were never going to get here,' she said.

'It won't be for a long time, Lu. But when I was making the cage in the carpenter's shop, Mr Baines was surprised how well I could handle the tools, and he said I can help him with repairs when he's really busy. So if I can work with him and learn, one day I'll be a real carpenter, like Father,' William said eagerly, his hand remembering the feel of a chisel.

'And we could really go back to Portsmouth?' she asked sleepily.

'When I can earn good money, we can go back.'

'Really? To the Cabin?'

'Well, I might have to build a new cabin some-where else,' William said, considering. 'I might even get a job on the Navy ships, like Father used—'

'Listen!' she interrupted. From under the bed came a rhythmic thrumming. Tigermouse had found her wheel. 'There's a good girl,' Lucy said happily.

'Go to sleep, Lu. You'll have to work hard tomorrow.'

After all the fun of the welcome party and riding Montague, he was afraid her first routine day would be something of a shock. But Lucy had it all worked out.

'Work with Will,' she murmured. 'Work... with...'

Then she fell fast asleep, hair spread over the pillow, clutching his thumb. He could have tiptoed away, but William went on sitting there a long time in the candlelight, deeply content with the present but dreaming of the future. Screaming gulls swept across a blue sky, small boats plied to and fro, the air smelled of seaweed and tar and a great ship, with white sails flying, sailed into the shining harbour, coming home to Portsmouth.

Historical Note

On the morning of 29 August 1782, a vast fleet of Royal Navy ships lay anchored in the Solent and Spithead, the sheltered stretch of water between the Isle of Wight and the mainland, being prepared to sail to the Mediterranean and relieve the garrison of Gibraltar, which was under siege by the Spanish and French. The fleet included thirty-six battleships, of which the largest were the *Victory* and the *Royal George*, which had just been refitted in Plymouth.

Captain Waghorn had ordered a repair to be made to a watercock, which let in seawater when required, for cleaning the ship. As this was below sea level, the ship was to be heeled over at an angle, for the cock to come within reach of the carpenter. To achieve this, the port guns were run out to the side while the starboard guns were drawn back. William Nickelsen, Master Attendant of Portsmouth Dockyard, had warned Admiral Kempenfelt that this was a dangerous plan with the ship already heavily laden for the voyage, but the Admiral had paid no heed.

While the carpenter was making his repair, he noticed that the ship was leaning further and further to starboard. It was he who rushed to the gun deck to give the first alarm, but it was too late—the *Royal George* heeled right over and sank, taking some twelve hundred people, crew, visitors and suppliers, with her.

A court martial held on board HMS *Warspite* declared the ship had rotten timbers so that her bottom had fallen out: this was to prevent the disgrace of Captain Waghorn and Admiral Kempenfelt. The Navy Board resisted all efforts to salvage the ship, which would have revealed her to be intact, but some of her cannon were later salvaged and melted down to form the base of Nelson's Column in London.

FEAR IN THE GLEN

Jenny Robertson

'Chosen and favoured and gifted, they say. Oh, child, be careful!' said Winnag the wise woman.

Bel's determination to improve her family's fortunes has put her in danger. It has brought her to the notice of the priests of the glen. Now they are seeking a sacrifice, and Bel is the Chosen One.

She is sure that Columba, the gentle yet powerful lord from Ireland, will be able to help. But no one knows where he is, and time is running out . . .

ISBN 0 7459 1874 3

GREYBACK

Eleanor Watkins

Edwin's life has been full of excitement since the Normans arrived, bringing many changes to the manor of Penwold. They have also given him Greyback, the offspring of a wolf and a sheep-dog, and Edwin's constant companion. Although many cannot believe that Greyback has forsaken the wild, he is tolerated by most people. But not everyone has accepted the Norman presence, and Edwin appears a traitor to some.

Unexpectedly separated, both boy and dog are faced with hard choices between the old ways and the new. Where do their true loyalties lie?

ISBN 0 7459 1409 8

More stories from LION PUBLISHING for you to enjoy: